The
Seven-Per-Cent
Solution

Little could Dr. Watson believe that the pathetic figure huddled before him was the great detective, Sherlock Holmes. Alas, it was his old friend Holmes, but a Holmes in bondage—not to any archvillain—but to a 7% solution of cocaine and sterile water. Driven by the drug to wild ravings, Holmes had to be duped into rehabilitation—before it was too late. . .

THE SEVEN-PER-CENT SOLUTION

"IS ONE HUNDRED
PER CENT PLEASURE"*

"Holmes and Freud working in double-harness, the psychoanalyst exploring the mental depths while Holmes observes and deduces . . . The climax is a double-hung doozer that will have you goggle-eyed . . . The book is a corker!"   —*Providence Journal*

"Intrigue, genius and pleasure . . . This book has them all!"   —*Raleigh News and Observer*

"It's great!"   —*Cleveland Plain Dealer*

"Don't miss it!"   —*Milwaukee Journal*

"It's a real shocker when the truth about Holmes is revealed!"

          —*The New York Sunday Times Book Review*

The Seven-Per-Cent Solution

*Being a Reprint
from the Reminiscences of
John H. Watson, M.D.*

as edited by

Nicholas Meyer

BALLANTINE BOOKS · NEW YORK

Library of Congress Catalog Card Number: 74-4018

ISBN 0-345-29814-4

This edition published by arrangement with E. P. Dutton & Co., Inc.

Printed in Canada

First Ballantine Books Edition: August 1975
Tenth Printing: January 1981

For Sally

Contents

ix

CONTENTS

Foreword

The discovery of an unpublished manuscript by John H. Watson may well engender in the world of letters as much skepticism as surprise. It is easier to conceive of the unearthing of one more Dead Sea Scroll than yet another text from the hand of that indefatigable biographer.

Certainly there has been a surfeit of forgeries—some of them admittedly well done and others merely preposterous—so that the appearance of one more supposedly authentic chronicle may automatically arouse bored hostility in the breasts of serious students of the Canon. Where did *this* one come from and why not before now? are the inevitable questions students are forced to pose time and time again, before going on to catalogue the myriad of inconsistencies in style and content that brand the piece a hoax.

For the present manuscript, it does not much matter whether or not I believe it to be genuine; for what it is worth, let me say that I do. As to how it came into my possession, that is frankly a matter of nepotism as the letter from my uncle, quoted in full below, will serve to indicate.

London, March 7th 1970

Dear Nick—

I know that both of us are busy so I'll come right to the point. (And you needn't worry, the enclosed bundle does not represent my attempt to make a stock-broker's life look glamourous and/or easy!)

Vinny and I bought a house in Hampshire three months ago from a widower named Swingline (if you can believe!). The poor man's wife had just passed on—she was only in her middle fifties as I understand it—and he was quite broken up; couldn't wait to leave the house. They'd lived in it since the war, and the subject of the attic was simply too painful to bear. All the effects and mementos and papers (how much one accumulates during a lifetime!) that he wanted were in the house proper, and he said if we didn't mind clearing out the attic ourselves, anything we found up there we could keep!

Well, it isn't always you get to rummage around in someone else's junk and take what you like but, to be truthful, the more I thought of doing it, the less enthusiastic I became. The place was jammed with furniture, bric-a-brac, standing lamps, dusty what-nots, and even old travelling steamer trunks (!), but there was something distasteful about going through poor Swingline's past—even with his permission.

Vinny, even though she felt the same way, is a homemaker. She wondered if there was anything we could use up there, furniture prices being what they are, and also she had items of our own she wanted to store out of the way. So up she went and down she came, choking with dust and smudged all over like a chimney-sweep.

I won't bore you with all the details, but we found the enclosed, Xeroxed a copy, and are sending it on to you. Apparently the late Mrs. Swingline was a typist (her maiden name being Dobson), and in that capacity she worked at the Aylesworth Home, an old folks' affair recently taken over by National Health (hurrah, hurrah). In the course of her work—which included helping the patients write letters—she transcribed onto her typewriter (also in the attic, by the by, and in mint condition) the enclosed, which was dictated to her—he states so himself—by one "John H. Watson, M.D."!!!

It took me a while to read the thing and I was three pages or more into what he calls his "Introductory" before I realized what the hell it was. Of course it occurred to me the whole thing might be some sort of incredible hoax, a hoax that never came off and got buried in an attic, so I checked into it. In the first place, Swingline knew nothing about it. I asked him casually and he didn't recall it at all, much less express any interest. Then I went to Aylesworth Home and asked them to check the files for me. There was some question about whether they were still accurate that far back—the war messed up everything—but my luck held good. In 1932 a Dr. John H. Watson was admitted (with severe arthritis), and it stated in his health record that he had been attached to the Fifth Northumberland Fusiliers! There could no longer be any doubt, at least in my mind, and I would fain have looked at the record in detail (wouldn't you have liked to know where Watson was *really* wounded?) but Matron wouldn't let me. She hadn't the time to stand around, she said, and the file was confidential. (Ah, bureaucracy, what would National Health do without you?)

Anyway, it offers substantial confirmation as to the authenticity of the enclosed, which I am forwarding to you for whatever purpose you think best. You are the Sherlockian in the family and will know what to do with it. If it comes to anything we split the profits!!

Fondest regards to you,
Henry

PS: Vinny says we have to cut her in, too—she found it.

PPS: We are retaining the original MS. We'll see if Sotheby's is interested in auctioning it!

Authentic or not, the manuscript required editing, and preparing a definitive edition of Plutarch could not be more difficult than the problems posed by a newly unearthed text of Watson's. I corresponded extensively with Sherlockians too numerous to mention here; all of them proved invaluable, tireless in offering advice, comments, and insights regarding the newly discovered material. The only proper acknowledgement of the debt this book owes them is the book itself. I have, with their help, preserved as much of Dr. Watson's narrative as makes for a consistent story.

For reasons which are not definitely known, Watson never (to our knowledge) got to edit the manuscript. His own death, possibly, or the vagaries of the war prevented him. Therefore, in readying the work for publication, I have tried to function as I believe he would have. I have struck out redundancies. Old people have a tendency to repeat themselves, and although Watson's memory of events apparently remained intact, he was prone in his dictation to reiterate significant details. I have also eliminated digressions which he made from time to time when his mind appears to have strayed from the story and wandered unchecked into the intervening years. (These memories are themselves not without interest and in subsequent editions I shall no doubt include them in the form of appendices.) Knowing that footnotes are especially irksome in the course of a narrative, I have deliberately kept them to a minimum and made the necessary ones as informal as possible.

For the rest, I have left well enough alone. The doctor is an experienced hand at telling a tale and needs no help from me. Aside from succumbing to the irresistible temptation to telescope or streamline an awkward phrase here and there (which the good doctor no doubt would himself have corrected in his revisions), all is as the faithful Watson set it down.

Nicholas Meyer
Los Angeles
October 30th, 1973

Introductory

For many years it was my good fortune to witness, chronicle, and in some instances to assist my friend, Mr. Sherlock Holmes, in a number of the cases which were submitted to him in his unique capacity as a consulting detective. Indeed, in 1881,* when I committed to paper the substance of our first case together, Mr. Holmes was, as he said, the world's *only* consulting detective. The ensuing years have seen that situation remedied to the satisfactory degree that today, in 1939, consulting detectives (if not actually known by that name) flourish both within and without the police contingent of nearly every country in the so-called civilized world. Many of them, I am gratified to see, employ the methods and techniques first developed by my singular friend so long ago—though not all of them are gracious enough to give his genius the wealth of credit it deserves.

---

* *A Study in Scarlet*, written by Watson after the case took place in 1881, was not published until December, 1887, when it appeared in the Beeton's Christmas Annual under the pen name A. Conan Doyle.

Holmes was, as I have always endeavored to describe him, an intensely private individual, reclusive in certain areas to the point of eccentricity. He was fond of appearing impassive, austere, and somewhat aloof: a thinking machine not in direct contact or communication with what he considered the sordid realities of physical existence. In truth, this reputation for coldness was deliberately and completely of his own manufacture. It was not, moreover, his friends—he admittedly had few—nor yet his biographer whom he sought to convince regarding this aspect of his character. It was himself.

The ten years since his death have provided me with ample time for reflection upon the question of Holmes's personality, and I have come to realize what I always really knew (but did not know that I knew)—that Holmes was a deeply passionate human being. His susceptibility to emotion was an element in his nature which he tried almost physically to suppress. Holmes certainly regarded his emotions as a distraction, a liability, in fact. He was convinced the play of feelings would interfere with the precision demanded by his work and this was on no account to be tolerated. Sentience he eschewed; those moments during his career when circumstances forced open floodgates of his reserve were rare indeed, and always startling. The observer felt he had witnessed a brilliant flash of lightning on a darkling plain.

Rather than indulge in such explosions—whose unpredictability threw him off balance as much as it did any witnesses—Holmes possessed a veritable arsenal of resources whose specific purpose (whether he acknowledged it or no) was to relieve emotional stress when such relief became imperative. His iron will having cauterized the more conventional outlets of expression, he would resort to abstruse and frequently malodorous chemical experiments; he would improvise by the hour upon the violin (I have stated elsewhere my admiration for his musical talents); he would adorn the walls of our residence in Baker Street with bullet pocks usually spelling out the initials of our gracious sovereign—the old Queen—or of some other notable whose existence was then calling itself to the attention of his restless mind.

Also, he took cocaine.

It may seem strange to some that I am beginning yet another chronicle of my friend's brilliant achievements in this roundabout fashion. Indeed, the fact that I am proposing to relate another history of his at this late date may seem strange in itself. I can only hope, before commencing my narrative, to explain its origins and to account for my delay in setting it before the public.

The origins of this manuscript differ sharply from those of past cases recorded by me. In those accounts I made frequent mention of the notes I kept at the time. No such notes were kept during the period occupied by the present narrative. The reasons for this apparent dereliction of duty on my part are two-fold. Firstly, the case commenced in so peculiar a manner that it was well under way before the fact was borne in upon me that it was actually a case at all. Secondly, once I realized what was happening I became convinced that it was an adventure which, for many reasons, should never see the literary light of day.

That I was mistaken in this assumption, the present manuscript happily bears witness. Fortunately, though I was morally certain that the occasion would never arise when I would find myself recording this history, the case is one which I have good reason to recall in almost every particular. I may say, in fact, that the fixtures of it are engraved in my memory and will be until my death and possibly after, though such metaphysics are beyond my competent speculations.

The reasons for the delay involved in setting this narrative before the public are complex. I have said that Holmes was a private person, and this is a case that cannot be set down without some exploration of his character, an exploration that would certainly have been distasteful to him when he was alive. Let it not be thought, however, that his being alive was the only obstacle. If that were true, there was nothing that should have prevented my writing this history ten years ago when he breathed his last amongst his precious Sussex Downs. Nor should I have felt qualms about writing the case "over his dead body," as I believe the phrase runs, for Holmes was notoriously sceptical about his reputation in the hereafter and entirely careless of the repercussions to his character on earth, once he himself had journeyed to that undiscovered country from whose bourne no traveller returns.

No, the reason for delay is that there was another party in the case, and it was esteem for this personage and a sense of delicacy on Holmes's part where this personage's reputation was concerned that caused him to enjoin me—under the strictest series of oaths—to disclose nothing of the matter until such time as this second party had also ceased to breathe. If that event did not occur before my own demise, then so be it.

Fate, however, has resolved the matter in favor of posterity. The party in question has died within the last twenty-four hours, and while the world resounds with eulogies of praise (and from some quarters, with utterances of damnation), while biographies and retrospectives are hastily printed and published, I—while I have still the strength of hand and clarity of mind (for I am eighty-seven and that is old)—likewise hasten to set down what I know no one else knows.

Such a revelation is bound to stir up controversy in several quarters, the more so as it involves my declaration that two of the cases I penned concerning Holmes were total fabrications. Attentive students of my writings have pointed out my apparent inconsistencies, my patent falsification of a name or a date, and have proved to the satisfaction of all that the man who wrote these cases down was a blundering fool, or, at best, an absent-minded dotard. Some more astute—or more charitable—scholars have suggested that my seeming errors were in fact deliberate sins of commission and omission, designed to protect or disguise the facts for reasons that were either obvious or known only to myself. It is not my intention here to enter into the lengthy process of correction and restitution of data. Let an apology suffice, and the timid explanation be advanced that when the cases were often set down in extreme haste, it chanced that I frequently chose what seemed to me to be the simplest way out of a difficulty imposed by the need for tact or discretion. In retrospect, this practise has proved more cumbersome than the truth would have been, had I been so bold, or in some cases so unscrupulous, as to write it.

Yet these same astute scholars mentioned earlier have never with a certainty branded as spurious the two cases which I spun almost entirely of whole cloth and have separated them from the others. I speak not here of forgeries by other hands than mine, which include such drivel as "The Lion's

Mane," "The Mazarin Stone," "The Creeping Man," and "The Three Gables."

I refer to "The Final Problem," with its account of the death duel between Holmes and his arch-enemy, the fiendish Professor Moriarty, and to "The Adventure of the Empty House," the companion case, which relates the dramatic reappearance of Holmes and details briefly his three years of wandering through Central Europe, Africa, and India, in flight from the minions of his deceased opponent. I have just re-read the cases and marvel, I must confess, at my lack of subtlety. How could attentive readers have missed my overbearing emphasis on "the truth" that I claimed to be telling? And what of all the theatrical flourishes in the prose, so much more to Holmes's taste than my own? (For though he protested his love of cold logic, he was at heart an unreconstructed dramatist of the most romantic and melodramatic turn.)

As Sherlock Holmes remarked on more than one occasion, evidence which seems to point unerringly in one direction, may, in fact, if viewed from a slightly altered perspective, admit of precisely the opposite interpretation. So, I venture to suggest, it is in writing as well. My repeated emphasis in "The Final Problem" on the undiluted truth which it contained should perhaps have aroused the suspicions of my readers and served to put them on their guard.

It is just as well, however, that nothing of the sort occurred, for secrecy, it will shortly be seen, was essential at the time. Now the real story may be told, the conditions stipulated by Holmes so long ago having at last been met.

I have remarked parenthetically that I am eighty-seven, and though I comprehend intellectually that I am in the general vicinity of death's door, yet emotionally I am as ill-equipped to grapple with oblivion as a man half or even a quarter of my age. Nevertheless, if the narrative which follows occasionally fails to bear the impress of my usual style, age must partly share the blame, along with the fact that years have elapsed since last I wrote. Similarly, a narrative which is not based on my usually copious notes is bound to differ significantly from previous works, however perfect my memory.

Another cause for variation is the fact that I am no longer actually writing—arthritis having made the attempt impossible—but rather dictating this memoir to a charming typist (a Miss Dobson), who is taking it down in some sort of coded abbreviation which she will subsequently transcribe to English—or so she promises.

Lastly, my style may appear dissimilar to that of my earlier writing because this adventure of Sherlock Holmes is totally unlike any that I have ever recorded. I shall not now repeat my earlier mistake and attempt to overbear the reader's scepticism by stating that what follows is the truth.

John H. Watson, M.D.
Aylesworth Home
Hampshire, 1939

PART 1
The Problem

1

Professor Moriarty

As I stated in the preamble to "The Final Problem," my marriage and my subsequent start in private practise wrought a subtle but definite alteration in the pattern of my friendship with Sherlock Holmes. At first his visits to my new home were regular and it was not infrequent that I repaid these calls with brief sojourns at my old Baker Street digs, where we sat before the fire, smoked a pipe or two, and Holmes caught me up on his latest investigations.

Soon, however, even this arrangement underwent a change; Holmes's visits grew increasingly sporadic and their duration lessened. As my practise increased, it became a matter of greater difficulty to manage my reciprocations.

During the winter of '90–'91, I saw him not at all and only learned from the papers that he was in France on a case. Two notes from him—dated Narbonne and Nîmes, respectively—were all the information he volunteered upon the subject, and they were terse, showing me that his time was demanded elsewhere.

A wet spring served to increase yet again my little but sturdy practise and it was well into April without a word from Holmes in many months. It was April 24th, in fact, and I was just clearing out the day's debris from my consulting room (not yet being in the position to afford the luxury of a clerk), when into it stepped my friend.

I was astonished to see him—not, I hasten to add—because of the lateness of the hour (for I was used to his odd comings and goings), but because of the change in him. He seemed thinner and paler than usual, which was thin and pale indeed, for he was habitually gaunt and white. His skin had a positively unhealthy pallour and his eyes were without their usual twinkle. Instead they roved restlessly in their sockets, aimlessly taking in their surroundings (it seemed) and yet registering nothing.

"Have you any objection to my closing your shutters?" were almost the first words out of his mouth. Before I could answer he edged his way quickly along the wall and, with an abrupt effort, flung closed and securely bolted the shutters. Fortunately there was a lamp burning in the room, and by its light I saw beads of perspiration trickling down his cheeks.

"What is the matter?" I asked.

"Air guns." He drew out a cigarette and with twitching hands was fumbling in his pockets for a vesta. I had never known him to be so jumpy.

"Here." I lit the cigarette for him. He looked at me keenly for a moment over the wavering flame, no doubt discerning my surprise at his behaviour.

"I must apologize for calling so late." He sucked the smoke in gratefully, his head thrown quickly back. "Is Mrs. Watson in?" he went on before I had time to digest his apology. He was pacing about the small room now, oblivious to my stares.

"She is away on a visit."

"Indeed! You are alone?"

"Quite."

He ceased pacing as abruptly as he had begun, looked at me, and softened his expression in response to mine.

"My dear fellow, I owe you an explanation. I have no doubt you find this all very bizarre."

I confessed as much and suggested he come with me to the fire and share a brandy, if that were possible. He considered the proposal with an air of concentration that would have been comical had I not known him to be a man who is never upset by trifles. At last he agreed, stipulating only that he must sit on the floor with his back to the mantel.

In the sitting room, having restoked the fire and settled us with our drinks—I in my armchair and Holmes upon the floor next to the blaze—I waited for him to satisfy my curiosity.

"Have you ever heard of Professor Moriarty?" he asked, plunging headlong into the business after a sip or two of his drink.

I had, in fact, heard the name, but did not say so. Moriarty was the appellation I had sometimes known him to mutter when he was deep in the throes of a cocaine injection. When the drug's effects had left him, he never alluded to the man, and, though I thought of asking him about the name and what significance it held for him, there was something in Holmes's manner that usually precluded such an enquiry. As it was, he knew how heartily I disapproved of his loathesome habit, and this was a difficulty I did not wish to exacerbate by referring to his behaviour while under its influence.

"Never."

"Aye, there's the genius and the wonder of the

thing!" He spoke with energy though without shifting his position. "The man pervades London—the Western world, even!—and no one has ever heard of him." He then astounded me by launching into an all-but-endless monologue on "the professor." I listened with growing wonder and apprehension as Holmes described for me his evil genius, his nemesis, as he called him. Forgetting the danger from the air guns (though he would have made a difficult target in my drawing room at that hour and in that light), he got to his feet and, resuming his restless pacing, detailed for me a career steeped in every kind of depravity and horror.

He told me that Moriarty had been born into a good family and had had an excellent education, being endowed by nature with a phenomenal mathematical faculty. At the age of twenty-one he had written a treatise upon the Binomial Theorem, which had enjoyed a lengthy European vogue. On the strength of it he had won the mathematical chair at one of our smaller universities. But the man possessed hereditary tendencies of the most diabolical kind, crossbred with his incredible mental prowess. It was not long before dark rumours gathered round him in the university town and eventually he was compelled to resign his chair and come down to London, where he set up as an army mathematical coach.

"That was merely a subterfuge." Holmes leaned into my face, resting his hands on the back of my chair. Even in the dim light I could perceive the pupils of his eyes dilating with unsteady intensity. The next instant he had resumed his infernal pacing.

"For years past, Watson, I have continually been conscious of some power *behind* the malefactor, some deep organizing power which forever stands in the way of the law and throws its shield over the wrong-doer. Again and again in cases of the most varying sorts—forgeries, robberies, murders—I have felt the presence of this force, and I have deduced its action in many of those undiscovered crimes in which I have not been personally consulted. For years I have endeavoured to break through the veil which shrouded it, and at last the time came when I seized my thread and followed it, until it led me, after a thousand cunning windings to ex-professor Moriarty of mathematical celebrity."

"But, Holmes—"

"He is the Napoleon of crime, Watson!" As my friend spun round from his position before the fire-place, the flames behind him and the shrill, un-natural quality of his voice lent his attitude a terri-ble aspect. I could see his nerves stretched to their highest limits. "He is the organizer of half that is evil and of nearly all that is undetected in this great city and in the annals of contemporary crime. He is a genius, a philosopher, an abstract thinker—he sits motionless, like a spider in the center of its web, but that web has a thousand radiations, and he knows well every quiver of each of them. His agents may be caught, they may be apprehended and their crimes forestalled—but he—*he* is never touched, never so much as suspected." *

And so he rambled on, sometimes incoherently, sometimes declaiming as if from the stage of the Old Vic. He listed crimes initiated by the profes-sor, he spoke of his system of safeguards designed to protect him from all suspicion or harm. He talked glowingly of how he, Holmes, had managed to penetrate that perimeter of the professor's de-

---

* All this tallies more or less with Watson's account of Holmes's opinion regarding Moriarty as set down in "The Final Problem."

fence and how the professor's minions, having discovered his success, were even now upon his track —with the air guns.

I listened to this erratic recital with mounting alarm, though I did my best to conceal it. I had never known Holmes to be untruthful and I could see at a glance that this was not one of his occasional practical jokes. He spoke in deadly earnest, almost babbling with fear. No human that I had ever heard of could match the catalogue of atrocities Holmes attributed to the professor. Irresistibly, I was reminded of Quixote's arch-foe, the Enchanter.

The tirade did not so much conclude as run down. From shrill statements Holmes gradually subsided into inarticulate mutterings and from thence to whispers. Accompanying this modulation in speech, his body, which had been striding energetically to and fro, now leaned up against a wall, then flung itself absent-mindedly into a chair and, before I realized what had happened, Holmes was asleep.

I sat in silence by the flames of the dying fire and studied my friend. Never had I known him to be in such deep trouble, but I was uncertain just what sort of trouble it was. From the way he spoke he almost seemed under the influence of some powerful narcotic.

Then an awful thought struck me. I recalled for the second time that night the only other occasions when I had known Holmes to talk of Moriarty. It was when he was deep in the spell of his cocaine.

Stealing quietly over to the chair where he lay slumped and obviously spent, I pulled back his lids and examined his pupils once again. I then took his pulse. It was weak and unsteady. I wondered if I might risk removing his jacket and examining his arms for recent puncture marks; but it was best not to risk waking him.

I resumed my chair and thought. In the past I had known Holmes to go on cocaine "binges," sometimes of a month's duration or more, during which time he would inject himself thrice daily with a seven-per-cent solution. Many readers have erroneously supposed that Holmes made use of our friendship so that I as a doctor might procure his supply of this terrible narcotic. Recently, I have even heard it postulated that my willingness to supply Holmes with his drug was the *only* reason he tolerated my companionship. Without pausing to comment on the patent absurdity of the suggestion, I will only note that Holmes had no such need. No statutes in the previous century prevented a man from purchasing cocaine or opium in whatever quantity he pleased. It was by no means illegal, and therefore my own reluctance or willingness to supply him with cocaine is quite beside the point. At any rate, there is ample record elsewhere of my own attempts to curb his vicious and self-destructive habit.

For certain periods, indeed, I had been successful—or, not I so much as my powers of persuasion in conjunction with the arrival of a new and absorbing case. Work was what Holmes craved, problems of the most challenging and perplexing nature were his element. Engaged upon a quest of this sort he had no need to resort to artificial stimulants of any kind. I seldom knew him to take more than wine with his dinner, and this, with the exception of huge amounts of shag,* was his only indulgence when involved with a case.

But challenging cases were rare. Was not Holmes

---

* Shag. A cheap, strong tobacco favoured by Holmes. Shag refers to the cut of the blend as well.

always lamenting the dearth of ingenuity among the criminal classes? "There are no great crimes anymore, Watson," had been his constant and bitter litany when we shared rooms together in Baker Street.

Was it possible that between the absence of intriguing misdeeds, and my own departure from Baker Street, Holmes had fallen prey once more—and this time beyond redemption—to the evils of cocaine?

Unless the fantastic tale he had just related to me turned out to be the truth, I could conceive of no other explanation that would cover the facts. It had always been a maxim of Holmes's that whenever the possible had been eliminated, the remainder—however improbable—was the truth.

With this thought I rose, knocked the ashes from my pipe against the grate, and, resolving to await developments, threw an afghan over the inert form of my companion and turned down the lamp.

I cannot be sure how much time elapsed in the darkness—an hour or two it must have been—for I was drowsing, myself, when Holmes stirred and woke me. For a moment I did not remember where I was or what had happened. Then, in a flash, I was recalled to myself and slowly turned up the gas.

Holmes was in the act of rising as well. For a moment he looked around with a blank air and I saw that he too had forgot where he was. Had he also forgot how he came to be there?

"A pipe and a snifter, eh, Watson?" he yawned contentedly in my direction. "Nothing like them on a wet spring night. Did you, too, surrender yourself into the arms of Morpheus as a result?"

I answered that it seemed I had, and then ventured to enquire after Professor Moriarty.

Holmes regarded me with a blank expression. "Who?"

I tried to explain that we had been talking of this gentleman before the effects of the brandy and the blaze in my hearth had made themselves felt.

"Nonsense," he replied testily. "We were discussing Winwood Reade and 'The Martyrdom of Man' and I was throwing in something or other of Jean-Paul. That's the last thing *I* remember," he added, looking at me significantly from under his brows. "If you remember otherwise I can only infer that your brandy is more potent than even its distillers claim."

I apologized and conceded that the memory was in fact my imagination, and, with a few more words, Holmes took his leave. He overrode my objections that it was hard on three in the morning.

"The night air will do me good, old man. And you know there is no one so experienced in getting about London at odd hours as myself. Thank Mrs. Watson for a pleasant evening, there's a good fellow."

I reminded him that my wife was in the country, whereat he looked at me sharply for a moment, then nodded, referred deprecatingly to the brandy again, and departed.

With grave misgivings, I bolted the door after him and ascended the steps to my own room, where I began disrobing, but then decided against it, and sat down in the chair next to the bedroom fire—which had long since gone out—with my hands on my knees.

For a while I even entertained the idea that Holmes had been right, that he had stopped over for the lag end of an evening, that we had smoked a pipe or two and downed a snifter or three, and that I had imagined all that talk of a Professor

Moriarty when, in fact, the conversation between us had occupied other channels entirely. Was that possible? In my present exhausted state I knew I was having as much trouble thinking clearly as a man does when he awakes from some vivid nightmare and for a season after cannot make himself realize that he is not still in hell.

I needed proof more tangible. Stealing downstairs again, carrying a lamp, I would have seemed a curious sight had the girl left her room and espied me: a middle-aged man with his boots off and his collar undone, creeping down the stairs of his own house with a befuddled expression on his face.

I entered the consulting room, scene of the commencement of this phantasy—if phantasy it was—and examined the shutters. They were closed and bolted, certainly. But who had closed them? Holmes, as I remembered him doing, or myself? Settled into my chair I tried to recall every detail of the conversation as I remembered it, pretending as best I could that I was Holmes listening to the deposition of a client in our old sitting room in Baker Street. The effect, had anyone chanced to be listening, would have been ludicrous enough. The middle-aged man without the boots was now sitting in a consulting room by the light of a single lamp and talking to himself—for I found it necessary from time to time to pose (as Holmes did) certain interrogatories concerning my own statement.

"Can you think of anything at all that the man said or did that you distinctly recall having covered in talk before the period when you both woke up and he spoke of the brandy you had drunk together?"

"No, I don't—stop a bit, though, I *do* remember something!"

"Excellent, Watson, excellent!" came the familiar phrase at my ear, only this time my own voice was speaking the words.

"He asked me when he first walked into the consulting room where Mary was. I told him she had gone visiting and that we were alone. Then later— after the nap we both took in our armchairs—he was on the point of leaving when he asked me to thank her for such a pleasant evening. I told him again that she was away and it startled him. He didn't remember my saying it earlier."

"You are quite certain you did mention it earlier?"

"Oh, yes, quite," I replied, a trifle miffed at the question.

"Then is it not possible, since we have allowed for the mellowing effects of the brandy already, that *he* forgot, simply forgot you had mentioned the fact before? Did he not, in fact, allude to that explanation himself at the time?"

"Yes, but—no, dash it all! We were neither of us in an alcoholic stupor!"

I got to my stockinged feet in my agitation and, seizing the lamp, padded into the sitting room again in an effort to leave my second voice behind.

Pulling back the curtains in the sitting room I saw that it must soon be getting light. I had been already fatigued when Holmes first appeared and now, it seemed, I was completely exhausted.

Had he appeared, though?

This was an even madder notion, and I cursed myself for having articulated it, even in the recesses of my brain. I turned from the window and the first light of dawn.

Of course, he had.

And for once I received proof positive of an assertion.

The two used brandy snifters lay where Holmes and I had left them.

I awoke the next morning, or rather that same morning, in my own bed, whither I had apparently flung myself half-dressed at some point during my profitless speculations of the night before. The house was already bustling with preparations for the day, and I arose with the intention of starting afresh, as it were, and seeing what came of that.

After changing and completing the process of dressing and shaving, I descended the stairs and had breakfast. Not even the papers were sufficient distraction: my mind was elsewhere already. I now recalled that I had taken Holmes's pulse and examined the pupils of his eyes the night before. But once again the same question came back to haunt me: had I really, or was this, too, part of the dream?

The question was too maddening to be endured, and, hastily concluding my breakfast, I went round to Cullingworth and asked him if he could see to my practise for the morning. He was happy to oblige (I had often assumed his at short notice), and without more ado I hailed a cab and set out for Baker Street.

It was still early in the morning when I stepped out onto the familiar stretch of pavement before 221B and paid the cabbie. I sucked in the morning air vigourously (for all that it was still rather damp), and rang the bell. The door was opened almost at once by our landlady, Mrs. Hudson. She seemed gratified beyond words to see me.

"Oh, Dr. Watson, thank heavens you've come!" she exclaimed without preamble, and astonished me by taking the sleeve of my coat and pulling me into the area-way.

"What is it—?" I began, but she cut me off with her fingers on her lips and looked anxiously up the stairs. Holmes's ears were of the keenest, however, and it was soon evident our brief exchange had been to some extent overheard.

"Mrs. Hudson, if that gentleman answers to the name Professor Moriarty," a shrill voice that was nonetheless recognizable as his called down from above, "you may show him up and I will deal with him! Mrs. Hudson?"

"You see how it is, Dr. Watson," the unhappy landlady whispered in my ear. "He's got himself barricaded in up there; won't take his meals, keeps the shutters closed all day—and then he steals out at night, *after* I've bolted the door and the slavey's in bed—"

"Mrs. Hudson—!"

"I'll go up and see him," I volunteered, patting her reassuringly on the arm, though in truth I did not feel particularly confident. So there *was* a Professor Moriarty, at least in Holmes's fancy. I mounted the seventeen well-trod steps to my old lodgings with a heavy heart. What a noble mind was here overthrown!

"Who is it?" Holmes enquired from the other side of the door when I knocked. "Moriarty, is that you?"

"It is I, Watson," I responded, and when I had repeated this several times, he at length consented to open the door slightly and peered at me strangely through the crack.

"You see it is only I, Holmes. Let me enter."

"Not so fast." His foot jammed against the base of the door. "You may be he disguised. Prove you are Watson."

"How?" I wailed, for I had no idea, in truth,

what it would require to satisfy him of my identity.

He thought for a moment.

"Where do I keep my tobacco?" he demanded abruptly.

"In the toe end of your Persian slipper." This answer, given so punctually, appeared to allay his suspicions to a degree, for his voice softened slightly.

"And my correspondence?"

"Is affixed to the mantel with a jack-knife."

He grunted an affirmation.

"And what were the first words I ever spoke to you?"

" 'You have been in Afghanistan, I perceive.' For heavens' sakes, Holmes!" I pleaded.

"Very well, you may enter," he replied, satisfied at last. He removed his foot from the door, opened it slightly, and pulled me in vigourously. The moment I had stepped across the threshold he closed the door behind me and threw several bolts and locks, none of which had ever been attached during my residence. I watched, transfixed, as he proceeded with these operations and then put his ear to the panel, listening for I knew not what. Finally, he straightened up and turned to me with an extended hand.

"Forgive me for doubting you, Watson," he said with a smile that was very like his own, "but I had to make sure. They will stop at nothing."

"The professor's gang?"

"Precisely."

He led me into the room and offered me tea which he had evidently brewed himself, using for the purpose the bunsen burner amidst his chemical apparatus on the deal table and a large beaker. I accepted a cup and sat down, looking about me, as Holmes went about pouring. The place was much the same as it had been when I shared it with him —it was as untidy as always—but the shutters and windows were bolted and the shutters themselves were not the ones with which I was familiar. They were new, constructed, as far as I could judge, of heavy iron. These and the many locks on the door were the only visible signs of alteration.

"Here you are, old man."

From his chair by the fire Holmes's arm jutted out as he passed me my teacup. He was wearing his dressing gown (the mouse-coloured one) and his bare arm protruded as he reached over.

It was a battlefield of puncture marks.

I will not detail the rest of that painful interview; its substance can be easily gleaned and it would cast an unworthy shadow on a great man's memory for me to relate what effects this horrible drug had produced upon his faculties.

After an hour I left Baker Street—being admitted to the outer world with almost as many precautions as I had been taken in from it—seized another cab, and returned to my own residence.

There, still reeling with the shock of Holmes's mental collapse, I encountered a disagreeable surprise. The girl, upon my entering, informed me that there was a gentleman waiting to see me.

"Didn't you inform the gentleman that Dr. Cullingworth was taking my rounds this morning?"

"Yes, I did, sir," she answered, ill at ease, "but the gentleman insisted on seeing you, personally. I didn't like to close the door on him, so I let him wait in the consultin' room."

This was really too much, I thought with rising irritation, and was about to say so when she came forward timidly with the salver in her hand.

"This is his card, sir."

I turned over the piece of white card-board and shuddered, the blood turning to ice in my veins. The name on the card was that of Professor Moriarty.

2

Biographical

For the better part of a minute I gazed stupidly at the card, and then, conscious of the girl's presence, thrust it in my pocket, handed her back the salver, and went past her into the consulting room.

I did not dare think. I did not want to think. I was incapable of thought. Let this—this gentleman—whoever he was, and whatever he called himself, explain matters to me if he could. I had, for the moment, no intention of speculating any further.

He rose at once as I opened the door, a small, shy personage in his sixties with his hat in his hand and a startled expression on his face that quickly subsided into a timid smile when I introduced myself. He extended a thin hand and took mine briefly. He was dressed well though not expensively, with the air of a professional man who is nevertheless unused to the hurly-burly of the real world. He belonged in a monastery, perhaps, where his blue myopic eyes would have no other business than to pore over ancient parchments and decipher their meanings. His head added to the monkish impression I had formed of his nature, for it was almost totally bald, with a few delicate wisps of white-grey hair circling the back and sides.

"I hope I have not inconvenienced you by occupying your consulting chamber," he was saying in a quiet but anxious voice, "only my business is of the most urgent and personal nature and it was you, not Doctor—ah—Cullingworth that I wished to—"

"Quite so, quite so," I interrupted with an asperity that I could see was startling to him. "Pray tell me what is the matter," I went on in a softer tone, and motioned him to sit down again as I drew up a chair opposite.

"I don't quite know how to begin." He had the disconcerting habit of turning his hat round and round in his hands as he spoke. I tried to imagine him as Holmes had described—a brilliant and diabolical fiend, sitting motionless at the center of every evil web of conspiracy spun by man. His appearance and attitude were not helpful.

"I have come to you," the professor resumed with sudden energy and decision, "because I know from reading your accounts that you are Mr. Sherlock Holmes's most intimate acquaintance."

"I have that honour," I acknowledged gruffly, with a perfunctory inclination of my head. I was determined to be on my guard, for though I judged his appearance to be innocuous I made up my mind that he would not deceive me by it.

"I am not sure how to say this," he went on, twisting his hat round more than ever, "but Mr. Holmes is—well, I suppose persecuting me is the only word to describe it."

"Persecuting *you?*" I ejaculated.

"Yes," he agreed hastily, starting again at the sound of my voice, though not apparently recognizing its emphasis. "I know it sounds absurd, but I don't know how else to put it. He—well, he stands outside my house at night—in the street." He stole a glance at me to see what reaction, if any, my features revealed. Satisfied that I was not about to erupt with indignation, he continued.

"He stands outside my house at night—not every night, mind you—but several times a week. He follows me! Sometimes for days on end he dogs my footsteps. He doesn't seem to mind my being aware of it. Oh, and he sends me letters," he added as an afterthought.

"Letters?"

"Well, telegrams, really; they're only a sentence or two. 'Moriarty, take care; your days are numbered.' Things like that. And he has seen the headmaster about me."

"The headmaster? What headmaster do you mean?"

"Headmaster Price-Jones, at the Roylott School where I hold the position of mathematics instructor." He had named one of the lesser-known public schools in the area of West London.

"The headmaster called me in and asked me to explain Mr. Holmes's allegations."

"And what did you tell him?"

"I said I was at a loss to explain them; I said I didn't know what they were. So he told me." Moriarty twisted round in his chair and screwed up his blue eyes in my direction. "Dr. Watson, your friend is persuaded that I am some sort of—" he groped for the words—"criminal mastermind. Of the most depraved order," he added with a helpless shrug, throwing up his hands. "Now I ask you, sir: in all honesty—can you see in me the remotest trappings of such an individual?"

There seemed almost no point in saying I could not.

"But what is to be done?" the little man pursued

with a whine. "I know that your friend is a good man—all England resounds with his praise. But, in my case, he has made some ghastly mistake and I have become his unfortunate victim."

Lost in thought, I said nothing.

"The last thing in the world that I would wish is to cause him any embarrassment, Doctor," the whine persisted. "But I am at my wits' end. If something is not done about this—this persecution, what other alternative have I than to turn the matter over to my solicitor?"

"That will not be necessary," I responded at once, though in truth I had no idea what course of action to follow.

"I sincerely hope it will not," he agreed. "That is why I have come to you."

"My friend has not been well," I answered, feeling my way. "This action is no part of his normal behaviour. If you had known him when he was in health—"

"Oh, but I did," interrupted the professor, to my vast surprise.

"You did?"

"I did indeed, and a most engaging young man he was, was Master Sherlock."

"Master Sherlock?"

"Why, yes. I was his tutor—in mathematics."

I stared at him open-mouthed. From the expressions succeeding one another across his own countenance, I gathered he had somehow assumed I knew this. I said I had not and begged him to tell me all about it.

"There isn't much to tell." The whine in his inflection was becoming disagreeably pronounced. "Before I came down to London—this was years ago, after University—"

"You didn't by chance write a treatise on the Binomial Theorem?" I interrupted.

He stared at me.

"Certainly not. Who has anything new to say about the Binomial Theorem at this late date? At any rate, I am certainly not the man to know."

"I beg your pardon. Please continue."

"As I was saying, I left University and accepted the position of tutor in mathematics in the home of Squire Holmes. There, I taught Master Mycroft and Master Sherlock——"

"I apologize again for interrupting you," I said, with great excitement, for Holmes had never spoken of his people to me in the entire period of our acquaintance. "Where was this?"

"Why, in Sussex, of course, at the family seat."

"The family was from Sussex?"

"Well, not originally. That is, the Holmes clan hailed from there, yes, but the Squire was a second son, never due to inherit the estate at all, by rights. He and his family lived in North Riding—in Yorkshire—that's where Master Mycroft was born. Then the Squire's elder brother died, a widower without issue, and Master Sherlock's father moved his family into the old estate." *

"I see. And that is where you met Holmes?"

"I taught both boys," Moriarty replied with more than a touch of pride, "and brilliant lads they were, too, both of 'em. I should have liked to go on,

---

* This statement would seem to reconcile the opposing views of the late W. S. Baring-Gould, who, in his biography of Holmes, postulated his Yorkshire background, with those of Trevor Hall, who more recently contended that Holmes was born and reared in east Sussex. Baring-Gould also informs us that Moriarty tutored Holmes in mathematics. How he came by this crucial piece of intelligence—without access to the present mss—he does not explain.

only—" he hesitated, "then came the tragedy—"

"Tragedy, what tragedy?"

Again, he favoured me with a bewildered glance. "Don't you know—?"

"Know? Know what, man? Good heavens, speak plainly!" I was on the edge of my chair with excitement. These details were so new to me that I fairly forgot the Holmes of the present, and his grave troubles, in my eagerness to satisfy my own curiosity about the Holmes of the past. Every word this little man uttered on the subject proved more astounding than the last.

"If Master Sherlock hasn't told you about it, I don't know that it is for me to—"

"But, see here—"

I could not convince him. He took the view that it was a professional confidence of sorts and nothing I could say on the subject would change his mind. The more urgently I pressed him the more reticent he became, until at last, deaf to my entreaties, he rose and looked about for his blackthorn.

"Really, I have said all that I came to say," he insisted, avoiding contact with my eyes as he fumbled for the stick. "You really must excuse me—no, I cannot and will not be indiscreet in this matter. I have told you all I can, and I leave it in your hands to resolve this—this dilemma."

He departed with a resolve for which I should have scarcely given him credit. Timidity was suddenly overcome by an anxiety for egress, and Professor Moriarty took his leave, allowing me to ponder my next move. Considering these tantalizing references to Holmes's past, replete with obscure tragedies, I privately felt that what the professor viewed as tragic might to myself appear merely sad, his being, as I suspected, an overly sensitive nature. But I had no time for these avenues of thought, however, so engrossed was my mind with the present predicament of Holmes's collapse and Moriarty's veiled threat (understandable under the circumstances, it grieved me to admit), of calling in his solicitor. This was to be avoided at all costs. Holmes's was a high-strung nature (I had known him to collapse before, though not, indeed, as a result of cocaine), and such an exposure was unthinkable.*

Rather, what he needed, I decided upon reflection, was therapy. His terrible habit must be broken, and for this I needed some kind of assistance, past experience having shown me that I was not capable of stemming his addiction with my own meagre resources and knowledge. Indeed, if I was correct, what I had scarcely managed before would prove quite impossible now. During the intervening months when our contact had been of the slightest, the fatal compulsion had increased its attractions ten-fold, so that now he was more in its awful grip than he had ever been. If I had been unable to help him break that grip before, when it was but a momentary grasp, how should I prevail now that it had become a stranglehold?

I looked at my watch and noted that it was almost two. With the better part of the day gone by, it would be foolish to resume my practise, for Mary would be returning from Mrs. Forrester's at five and it was my intention to be at Waterloo by then to meet her.

In the meanwhile I would go to Bart's and seek out Stamford's advice—not telling him, of course, the entire truth, but setting the problem before him as belonging to one of my own patients.

---

* Watson mentions two instances of such a collapse, in "The Reigate Squires" and in "The Adventure of the Devil's Foot."

Stamford, it may be recalled, had been a dresser under me at Bart's when I was studying at the University of London back in '78. Since then, he had gone on to take his own degree at that same august institution and was now a physician on staff at the old hospital where, so many years ago—in the chemical laboratory—he had first introduced me to Sherlock Holmes. He did not know Holmes well and had only brought us together when he learned we were each of us desirous of finding and sharing good rooms at a reasonable price. I did not intend to allude to Holmes today if I could help it.

Once again I set out from my home, this time with some bread and cold ham, supplied by the girl, which I wrapped in paper (over her protestations) and stuffed in my pocket as I had seen Holmes do so often, when, being engaged upon a case, he had no time for a more conventional repast. The memory caused a pang in my breast as I climbed into a cab and started off for Bart's on my dismal errand.

It has been wondered at by contemporary scholars that Holmes and I were so fond of cabs, which admittedly were dear, when the Underground was to be travelled for considerably less. As long as I am clearing up mysteries, I may say that though the Underground was less expensive than the horse-drawn vehicles we favoured, and though it was in some instances definitely faster, it is also true that the lines were not completed and in many cases did not take us where we wished to go.

But the real reason we did not use them when we could avoid it (and "we" here is meant to include most gentlemen of means) was that the Undergrounds at that time were a hell beneath the earth. Steam-driven, filthy, sulphurous, and danger-ous, they were unreliable when they were not lethal and no fit place for a human who could afford another mode of locomotion. People who were forced to use them inevitably suffered lung ailments, and my practise, which bordered on the railway, saw many workmen, builders, and maintainers of that subterranean network of trains, who may be said to have literally given their lives so that Londoners today might enjoy the safest and most modern system of cheap transport in the world.

No Underground connected Baker Street with Bart's—in 1891 Baker Street was nowhere near the length it is today—and so a cab was not an extravagance but a necessity (unless one considered the omnibuses, but they had their own imperfections).

St. Bartholomew's must rank as one of the oldest hospitals in the world. Its twelfth-century structure was erected on Roman foundations, supposedly by Henry I's jester, Rahere, who, on a pilgrimage to Rome caught sick and swore—if he should recover—to build a great church in London.* I know not if the tale is true, but Bart's did begin as a church and remained one until Henry VIII annexed it in the name of the Crown and then proceeded (as he did elsewhere) to destroy much of the ecclesiastical portions of the building, suffering the hospital itself to be only slightly altered in the transition. Until some twenty years before I studied at Bart's, the great Smithfield Market with its huge slaughterhouses was right by the way, and the stench of dead animals was said to quite overpower every other odor for miles around. I am glad that before I ever arrived Smithfield had been dis-

---

* For a detailed description and history, see Michael Harrison's excellent volume, *In the Footsteps of Sherlock Holmes*, Drake Publishers.

banded, and, where animals once shrieked their death agony and blood ran thick in gutters, a number of goodly public houses and shops had risen in its place. I am told it is more or less unchanged to this day, but I have not returned to Bart's this last fifteen years.

When I entered its portals in my cab that April 25th, however, I thought not of the ancient building's lineage, nor did I halt to peruse the hodgepodge of architectural additions and encrustations that alternately delight and infuriate the eye. I paid off the cab and went straight into the Pathological Department and sought out Stamford.

My journey took me through a veritable labyrinth of corridors and turnings, forcing me to ask directions several times, so long had it been since I last threaded the maze. There was no reeking odor of Smithfield now. Instead, my nostrils were assailed by the pungent fumes of carbolic and alcohol, nothing new to them, since those twin harbingers of the medical profession accompanied me daily on my rounds. Nonetheless, their concentration was admittedly great here at Bart's.

Stamford, it developed, was giving a lecture, and I was obliged to take a seat at the back of the high-tiered auditorium and wait for him to conclude. It was hard, indeed, to concentrate on his words —something about circulation, I fancy, though I am not prepared to swear to it—so distracted was I with my own purposes. Nevertheless, I do recall looking down at him, standing on the rostrum as though he owned it, and remembering how long it had been since he and I had sat in these very seats and listened to yet another revered curmudgeon dinning these same facts into our own thick skulls. Stay, was Stamford not already beginning to resemble that curmudgeon? Whatever was his name?

When the talk was finished I strode down to the front and called to him as he neared the door.

"Great heavens, it's Watson!" he cried, stepping over to me at once and vigorously wringing my hand. "What on earth brings you to Bart's on this of all days? Heard my talk, did you? I wager you didn't think I could remember all that foolishness. Have you?"

And so he chattered on for several minutes, and, taking me by the arm, led me through additional sections of labyrinth to his own office, which was spacious but cluttered with the double paraphernalia of a physician who is also a teacher. Stamford had a jolly way with him as a youth and it pleased me to see that he still rattled on as mindlessly as ever. He had aged gracefully, and possessed the same old good-humoured air without his previous plumpness; his harried professional manner also became him—it gave him something to joke about, and yet he was sufficiently busy so as not to be wholly distracted by his propensity for being "clever," as he put it.

I let him ramble away for a decent interval, supplied him with details of my own life, my marriage, budding practise, and so forth, and dealt as best I could with the inevitable queries about Holmes.

"Who would have ever thought you two would hit it off so splendidly?" he chortled, and offered me a cigar which I accepted. "And you—you've become almost as notorious as he! what with your accounts—'Study in Scarlet,' 'Sign of the Four'— you've a real gift for telling a tale, Watson, and a flair for titles, too, I'll be bound. Tell me, now—we are quite alone and I'll never breathe it to a soul— can your friend and mine, can old Holmes really do all the things you've said he does in those accounts of yours? Truly now!"

I answered coldly that in my opinion Sherlock Holmes was the best and wisest man I had ever known.

"Quite, quite," Stamford rejoined hastily, perceiving at once his want of tact. Then he leaned back in his chair. "Who'd've thought it? I mean I always knew the man was clever but I'd no idea—! Well, well, well." He seemed at last to realize that I had come to visit him with some definite end in view, and he now turned his attention to it. "Was there something I could do for you, old man?"

I said there was, and, collecting myself, briefly outlined for him the case history of a patient in the thrall of cocaine, alluding tactfully to the phantasies that accompanied the heavier stages of the addiction. I asked him what steps could be taken to cure the man of his suffering.

Stamford, to do him justice, listened to me with perfect attention, his hands on his desk, smoking in silence, as I unfolded the details.

"I see," he said, when I had done. "And tell me, do you mean to say that the patient himself is not aware of the origins of this feeling—that someone is out to do him harm? He does not understand that this delusion is fostered by the drug he persists in using?"

"Apparently not. I believe it has got to the stage —if this is possible—when he is no longer aware of taking the cocaine at all."

Stamford shot up his eyebrows at this, then blew air soundlessly out of his cheeks.

"I will be candid with you, Watson. I don't know if that is possible or not. In point of fact," he continued, rising and coming round his desk to me, "the medical profession knows very little about addiction of any kind. Yet, if you have kept up your reading, you are aware that at some point in the not-too-distant future, such drugs as cocaine and opium are likely to be declared illegal without prescription."

"That will scarcely be of any use to me," I cried bitterly. "By that time my patient may well be dead." The thought caused my voice to rise in a manner that attracted his attention. I must be more off-hand.

Stamford studied me for a moment, and I withstood his scrutiny as best I could. Then he returned to his chair.

"I don't know what to tell you, Watson. If you were able to convince your—your patient that he must place himself totally under your supervision and care—"

"Out of the question," I interrupted, managing casually to wave my cigar about.

"Well, then—" he threw out his hands in a helpless gesture. "Wait a bit, though." He rose from his chair again. "There was something here that might be of use to you. Now where did I put it?"

He began rummaging about the office, carelessly disturbing piles of papers and causing a deal of dust to rise about us. With another pang I was reminded of Holmes's own chaotic filing arrangements at Baker Street, where finding a reference or looking up an old case was likely to send both of us coughing into the street for an hour or two while dust settled.

"Here it is!" he exclaimed in triumph, and he heaved himself erect from a floor-level cabinet by the window, holding in his hands a copy of *Lancet*.

"This is March 10," he said, handing it to me and catching his breath. "Have you seen it?"

I said I had not, my practise was keeping me so busy, but I believed I had it at home.

"Well, take this with you anyway in case you've misplaced your copy," Stamford insisted, pressing it into my hands. "There's a young chap—in Vienna, I think it is—at any rate, I didn't have time to read

the whole thing, but it seems he's involved in con-
ducting cocaine cures. I can't remember the name
but it's in there somewhere and maybe he says something that can be of help. I'm sorry, old man, but
I'm afraid it's the best I can do."

I thanked him profusely and we parted with many
promises on both sides to dine together in the near
future, to introduce one another to our wives, and
so forth. We had neither of us the slightest intention
of carrying out these extravagant proposals, and
my heart was in my boots as I set out for Waterloo.
I had no more faith than Stamford that the little
piece in *Lancet* could save my friend and bring him
back from the abyss into which he had fallen. Little
did I dream, as I set off to meet my wife, that for
the second time in ten years, Stamford—priceless,
invaluable Stamford!—had answered my prayers,
and Holmes's.

3

A Decision Is Reached

"Jack, dearest, whatever is the matter?"

These were my wife's first words to me as I handed her down from the train at Waterloo. There was between us a great spiritual bond which had first manifested itself the night we met, three years before.* Drawn together by circumstance in a tangled skein of people and events that included escaped convicts, Andaman Island savages, retired and ruined army officers, the Great Mutiny and the fabled Agra treasure, we two had stood together in the darkness that awful night on the ground floor of Pondicherry Lodge, whilst Sherlock Holmes and the housekeeper had gone upstairs with Thaddeus Sholto and there discovered the body of his unfortunate brother, Bartholomew. On that

---

* Much controversy has raged amongst scholars concerning Watson's marriage, or marriages. Without entering into the question of how many times he was married, and to whom, this passage and the one that follows it makes it perfectly clear that the woman to whom he refers was Mary Morstan, Holmes's client in "The Sign of the Four" and the only female Watson positively states he married.

41

ghastly occasion, without a word being spoken—
without, in fact, our knowing one another at all—
our hands had instinctively groped for one another's
in the gloom and clasped. Like two frightened
children, we sought at the same time to comfort
one another, so quick was the sympathy between us.

That lively and intuitive understanding persisted
until the day of her death. Certainly it was in
evidence when she stepped off the train that evening
in April and gazed anxiously into my face.

"What is it?" she repeated.

"Nothing. Come, I will tell you when we are
at home. Is this all your luggage?"

And so I diverted her attention for the moment
as we threaded our way through the crowded
station, weaving in and out amongst trunks, portmanteaus, bellowing porters, and parents endeav-
ouring to keep track and control of squalling off-
spring. Somehow we negotiated the hubbub, located
a cab, paid off our own porter (once our luggage
was strapped on high), got in, and left behind us
that scene of perpetual chaos which was Waterloo.

Once we were settled and on our way, my wife
attempted to resume her questions, but I resisted
them, chatting idly and putting forth a determinedly
cheerful countenance. I asked her how she had
enjoyed her visit with her former employer, for
she had occupied the position of governess in the
home of Mrs. Forrester when I had first been so
fortunate as to make her acquaintance.

She was puzzled at first by my obstinacy, but
seeing there was nothing for it, fell in with my
wish and gave me a lively account of her stay at
the Forresters' country home in Hastings, and of
the children, her former charges, who were now
quite old enough to dispense with governesses
altogether.

"Or so they would like to think," my wife amended with a laugh. I think I never loved her more than I did during that ride. She knew I was upset by something, but, seeing I did not then wish to communicate it, she took her cue from my questions and humoured me with the perfectest grace until I had nerved myself to face the ordeal. She was an excellent woman and I miss her cruelly to this day.

Supper was waiting for us when we arrived, and we went through the meal affecting the same light-hearted banter, each attempting to regale the other with anecdotes and incidents that had occurred whilst we were apart. As the repast drew to a close, however, she sensed the subtle transition in my mood, and anticipated me.

"Come, Jack, you've beat about the bush long enough. You cannot possibly be interested in further details of those horrid children. Now take me into the sitting room," she went on, rising and stretching forth her hand, which I took instantly. "There's a fire there waiting to be lit. Then we shall make ourselves comfortable and you shall have a brandy and soda if you wish it, with your pipe. Then you will tell me what has happened."

I followed my wife's directions as meekly as a child, except that I did not put any soda in my brandy. My wife had been impressed, in the early days of our acquaintance, with my portrait of General Gordon. How she came to possess the following trivial piece of information I never discovered (very possibly as she came from a military background it was common knowledge), but General Gordon was said to favour the brandy and soda above all other concoctions. My wife, perhaps because I had been wounded in action in Afghanistan, held an exaggerated notion of my affiliations with the army. She was forever attempting to cultivate in me a taste for General Gordon's brew. In vain I protested that I had inherited the general's picture on the death of my elder brother; in vain protested that the general had never commanded the Fifth Northumberland Fusiliers. She revered him to distraction, primarily for his work in ending the Chinese slave trade; and she never abandoned hope that I should some day come to relish her hero's drink. Tonight, however, she did not sulk when she perceived that I had—as was my custom—omitted the soda from my glass.

"Now, Jack," she prompted, having arranged herself very prettily on the horse-hair sofa opposite the chair in which I sat—the chair in which Holmes had fallen asleep the night before. She was still in her travelling costume—grey tweed with a touch of lace at the wrists and throat—though she had removed her hat before supper.

I took a pull at my brandy, made a great show of lighting my pipe, and then related the entire catastrophe.

"Poor Mr. Holmes!" she cried at the end, clasping her hands together in agitation, tears standing in her eyes. "What are we to do? Is there anything we can do?" Her readiness and willingness to help warmed my heart. She had no thought of shunning the difficulty, of avoiding my companion and the sordid disease that had overtaken and distorted his true nature.

"I think there *is* a measure that may be tried," I answered, getting to my feet, "but it will not be easy. Holmes is too far gone to accept help willingly and I daresay he is still too clever to be tricked into applying for it."

"Then—"

"A moment, dearest. I wish to fetch something from the hall."

I left her briefly, and retrieved the copy of *Lancet* Stamford had given me. I wondered, as I walked back to the sitting room, whether or not Mary could help me, if necessary, to effect my plan. The plan had been slowly forming in my brain since I had sat on a bench in Waterloo waiting for her train, reading about the Austrian specialist.

I returned to the sitting room, closed the door, and told my wife of my interview with Stamford and what had come of it.

"You say you have read the article?" said she.

"Yes, twice, while waiting for your train." Resuming my chair, I spread the issue of *Lancet* open upon my knee as I thumbed through it in search of the piece.

"This doctor—ah, here it is—this doctor has made a thorough study of cocaine. He came to the early, and, he confesses, erroneous conclusion that its powers were miraculous, capable of curing almost any disease and of ending alcoholism. He discovered, however, the terrible curse of its addiction when a dear friend of his perished as a consequence."

"Perished," she echoed in hushed tones, speaking in spite of herself.

We looked at one another, fearfully, as the awful possibility of Holmes's death in this grotesque fashion assailed our imaginations. My wife, no less than I, had reason to be grateful to Holmes, for it was through his agency that we had come to meet. I swallowed and went on.

"At any rate, after the death of this chap (it happened earlier this year), the doctor who wrote this article reversed his endorsement of cocaine and now expends his energies in the hope of curing unfortunate folk who have come within its thrall. He knows more about the drug than anyone else in Europe."

Again, we exchanged glances.

"Will you correspond with him?" she asked.

I shook my head. "There is no time. Holmes is too far along the path to destruction to waste an hour. His constitution is strong, but it cannot withstand the ravages of the venom he administers to himself. Unless we get help for him at once, his body will fail before we are ever given the opportunity to repair his mind."

"Then what do you propose, Jack?"

"I propose taking him to the Continent. I propose letting this doctor work on him himself, while I attempt to render every assistance that my knowledge of Holmes and my willingness to sacrifice time and energy can provide."

My wife sat silent for some moments in deep thought. When she turned to me again, the practical side of her nature asserted itself in a series of penetrating questions.

"Suppose the man can do no good—what then?"

I shrugged. "He is the only person in Europe who seems to know anything of the matter. What alternative have we but to try?"

She nodded.

"But what of the doctor? Will he see Holmes? Perhaps he is too busy, or—" she hesitated, "too dear."

"I shall be able to answer that question more accurately when I have an answer to my telegram," I told her.

"You sent a telegram?"

I had wired from Waterloo after reading the article. This was taking a leaf from Holmes, who preferred telegrams to all other forms of communica-

tion. I winced, remembering that he was at present
addressing them to poor Moriarty. My case, however, was justified. Nothing short of a telegram could
have served my purpose. As for the telephone,
even had overseas lines been available in '91 I
should not have used them. I had contracted from
Holmes his prejudice against the telephone. With a
telegram, as Holmes said, one is forced to be
concise, and, as a result, logical. Messages beget
messages in return, not a lot of useless gibbering.
I did not want a qualified or long response, just an
unadorned yes or no.

"Ah," my wife began, leaning back unhappily,
with a sigh, "but we have not reckoned with Mr.
Holmes himself. You admit that he is not to be
tricked into applying for help. Suppose the doctor
does accept him as a patient. How are we to get
him there? From what you have said, I understand
him to be more on his guard than ever."

"That is true," I replied, shaking my head. "It
will not be easy to get Holmes abroad. He must
be made to feel he is going of his own volition."

"And how are we to accomplish that?"

"He must be made to believe he is on the track
of Professor Moriarty—and we must provide the
clues."

My wife favoured me with the blankest stare of
astonishment I have ever beheld on a human countenance.

"Provide the clues?" she gasped.

"Yes." I held her eyes steadily with my own.
"We must plant a false trail that will lead Holmes
to Vienna."

"He will see through your scheme," she protested
automatically. "No one knows so much about clues
as does he."

"Very likely," I responded, "but no one knows

47

so much about Holmes as do I." I leaned forward.
"I will use every device I know will attract him, to
put him on the scent. Subtlety is not my forte, but
it is his. I shall absorb it temporarily. I shall think
like him; I shall consult my notes of past cases
he and I worked on together; you will help me;
and," I concluded, more bravely than I felt, "we
shall get him to do our bidding. If necessary," I
added lamely, "I am prepared to spend money as if
it were water."

My wife bent towards me and took my face
earnestly in both her hands. She gazed searchingly
but with affection into my eyes.

"You would do all this—for him?"

"I should be the most miserable wretch on earth
if I did not," I replied, "seeing what he has done
for me."

"Then I shall help you," said she simply.

"Good." I seized her hands in mine and pressed
them with excitement. "I knew I could depend upon
you. But first we must gain the cooperation of the
doctor."

That obstacle to our plans, however, was overcome momentarily. There was a knock at the front
door, and shortly thereafter the girl entered the
room with a telegram in her hand. With trembling
fingers I tore open the seal and read a brief message,
couched in quaintly awkward English, to the effect
that the doctor's "services were to the great English
detective gratis offered," and that he was anxiously
awaiting word. I scribbled a hasty reply and sent
the girl to the door with it.

Now all that remained was to get Sherlock
Holmes to Vienna.

4

Interlude in Pall Mall

Of course, it was one thing to say one was going to assimilate the mind of Sherlock Holmes and quite another to do it.

Fired by the telegram, we drew our chairs closer to one another, and, pausing only long enough for me to get my cases down from the shelves, set about planning our false trail.

Alas, it proved more difficult than even I had imagined. Students of my works have seen fit to remark that the man who wrote them was "slow," a dullard, hopelessly gullible, totally without imagination, and worse. To these charges I plead not guilty. While it is true that I have employed literary licence in recounting some of my adventures with Holmes, and have therefore sometimes erred in making myself appear too stupid in comparison, yet I included these exaggerations not for the mere sake of enhancing my friend's abilities in the eye of the reader, but rather because being in his company often made one feel dull whether or not he possessed a normal intelligence.

But when a normal brain, coupled with all the

good will in the world, sets out to dupe a superior one, it very quickly becomes evident where the problem lies. We made a dozen false starts that night, and each had some gap in it, some flaw in the reasoning, or else in its lack of the quality that I knew in advance would fail to engage Holmes's attention. My wife, playing devil's advocate, several times punctured what briefly appeared to be brilliant schemes.

How long I sat before the hearth, cudgeling my brains and poring over my notes, I know not, except that it seemed longer in my fancy than was subsequently borne out by the clock above the mantel.

"Jack!" exclaimed my wife abruptly, "we're going about this all wrong."

"How do you mean?" I demanded, somewhat nettled, for I was doing the very best I knew how and it irked me to hear from my own wife that my efforts in a dear friend's behalf were "all wrong."

"Don't be angry," she said quickly, perceiving the flush which spread over my features. "I only meant that if we want someone to outwit Mr. Holmes, we must go to his brother."

Why ever hadn't I thought of it before? I leaned forward impulsively and kissed my wife upon the cheek.

"You are right," said I, rising. "Mycroft is the very man who can bait our trap. Even Holmes admits that Mycroft is his intellectual superior."

In my haste I had already started towards the door.

"Will you go there now?" she protested. "It is nearly ten. Jack, you have done enough for one day."

"I tell you there is no time to be lost," I replied, slipping into my jacket, which had hung before the blaze. "Besides, if I can reach the Diogenes Club before eleven I may very possibly find Mycroft still there. You needn't stay up for me," I added, kissing her tenderly once more.

Outside, I hailed a hansom and told the driver to take me to the Diogenes Club, where Mycroft was usually to be found. This done, I reclined on the cushions and listened to the clip-clop of the horse's iron shoes against the cobblestones as we drove through the gas-lit streets. I tried to keep awake, though in truth I was fairly done up.

Nevertheless, I had known Holmes, when on a case, to be capable of the most superhuman exertions. If I was unable to emulate his brilliance, at least I could match his endurance.

I did not know Mycroft Holmes well. Indeed, I had met him only once or twice and that some three years earlier, when our paths had crossed during the unhappy business of the Greek interpreter. Indeed, I had been more than seven years in residence with Holmes before he mentioned having a brother, and the revelation astounded me as much as if I had learned the earth was flat. I was further amazed when Holmes indicated his brother's mental faculties were even keener than his own.

"Then surely," I said at the time, "he is an even greater detective, and, that being the case, how is it I have never heard of the man?" For it seemed impossible that another such brain as Holmes's could exist in England with no one remarking upon it.

"Oh," Holmes had replied airily, "Mycroft prefers to hide his light under a bushel, so to speak. He is very lazy," he added, seeing that I did not understand. "He would be perfectly willing to piece out a mystery if it did not involve getting out of his chair. Unfortunately there is often more to it than that," he chuckled, "and Mycroft abhors anything in the nature of physical exertion."

He went on to explain that his brother spent most of his time in the Diogenes Club, across from his lodgings in Pall Mall. The Diogenes was a club devoted to a membership that could not abide clubs. It contained the queerest and most unsociable men in London, and no member was on any account permitted to take the least notice of another member. Save only in the Stranger's Room, talking was strictly prohibited.

I had actually dozed off when the cabbie opened the trap and, without looking down, announced in an off-hand way that we had reached our destination.

Stepping quickly across the street to the club's entrance, I gave the footman my card and requested that he send Mr. Mycroft Holmes to me in the Stranger's Room. He bowed stiffly and retreated upon my errand. Only a flicker of his eye-lids, half-closed in perpetual hauteur, gave me to understand that he thought my appearance irregular. I made a feeble attempt to straighten my collar and passed a rueful hand over the bristle on my chin. Fortunately, there was no need to remove my hat and comb my hair. Though the custom was dying out even then, men—especially in clubs—often retained their hats indoors.

After an interval of five minutes, the steward rejoined me, walking on padded feet, and, with a graceful motion of his gloved hand, ushered me forth and deposited me in the Stranger's Room, where I found Mycroft Holmes.

"Dr. Watson? I wasn't sure I should recognize you." He waddled forward and took my hand in his pudgy fingers. I have stated elsewhere that in contrast to Sherlock's gaunt physique, his brother was fleshy to the point of obesity. The years had not diminished his girth that I could detect, and he, for his part, observed me narrowly out of pig-like eyes lost in folds of fat.

"You have some urgent business that concerns my brother, I perceive," he went on, "for you have been traveling all day in his behalf—using hansoms, I should judge—and you have stopped briefly at Waterloo to pick something—or, no," he amended, "to pick someone up. You are very tired," he added, indicating a chair. "Please tell me what has happened to my brother."

"How did you know anything has happened to him?" I asked, sinking into the chair with amazement. Here was Holmes's sibling indeed.

"Pooh," Mycroft waved an enormous paw. "I have not seen you these three years and then it was in the company of Sherlock, whose doings I know you chronicle. Suddenly you pay me a visit at a time when most married men are at home with their wives, *and* you arrive without your alter ego. It is an easy matter to suppose that something is amiss with him and you come to me for help or advice. I can see by your chin that you have been about all day with no opportunity to shave again, as your beard demands. You are not carrying your medical bag, though from your own statements in print I know you have resumed your practise. Therefore I conclude that your arduous business is connected with your visit to me this evening. The date of the visitor's stub projecting from the pocket of your ulster informs me that you have been on the platform at Waterloo today. If you had been there to collect a parcel you would not, of course, have needed to go further than the luggage room, for which, I believe, no visitor's pass is required; therefore you were at the station to meet someone. And as for the hansoms which have been carrying you about all day, your beard and haggard expression proclaim that you have not been home; yet your Ulster is dry and your boots are clean despite the inclement weather. And what other mode of transportation can effect this paradox so well as that which our Mr. Disraeli calls the gondolas of London? You see, it is all quite simple. Now tell me what has happened."

He drew up a chair opposite to mine, giving me time to digest my astonishment, smiled kindly, and offered me a drink. I shook my head.

"You have not been in touch recently with your brother, then?" I asked.

"Not for more than a year."

This did not seem strange to me, though most people would have thought it odd that two brothers living in the same city, with no quarrel betwixt them, should have kept so totally apart. But the Holmes brothers were the exception, not the rule, as I had good reason to know.

Cautioning Mycroft Holmes that my tidings were not pleasant, I told him of his brother's condition and how I proposed to remedy it. He heard me out in dejected silence, hanging his head lower and lower as I spoke. When I finished, the pause which followed was so long that for a moment I wondered if he had fallen asleep. A deep rumbling sigh almost persuaded me that he had, but it was followed by his head coming slowly up until his eyes were level with mine once more. Behind their piggy look I saw pain.

"Moriarty?" he repeated at last, huskily.

I nodded.

He cut me off with a weary wave of his hand.

"Quite so, quite so," he murmured, then lapsed again into silence, staring at his finger ends. At length, with another sigh, he heaved himself to his feet, and spoke with animation, as if attempting to throw off the depression into which my news had plunged him.

"Getting him to Vienna will not be easy," he agreed, going to the door and pulling the bell-rope, "but it should not be impossible, either. In order to do so we must merely persuade him that Moriarty is there—there and waiting for him."

"But that is precisely what I have no idea how to accomplish."

"No? Well, the simplest solution is to induce Professor Moriarty to go to Vienna. We'll need a cab, if you please, Jenkins," Mycroft Holmes said over my shoulder to the steward who had responded to the bell-rope's summons.

He was silent during our nocturnal journey to number 114 Munro Road (the Hammersmith address provided us by the professor's card), except that he enquired about the Austrian specialist and asked who he might be. I explained in some detail about the article in *Lancet,* and he responded with a grunt.

"Sounds Jewish," was his only comment.

I was getting a second wind, and having Mycroft —and Mycroft's brain—enlisted in my cause did much to restore my spirits. I was tempted to ask him about Professor Moriarty and the tragedy he had referred to, but I held my tongue. Mycroft was clearly preoccupied with the present plight of his brother; there was something in both their natures that seemed to preclude such presumption, even in a friend, and I was certainly no intimate of Mycroft's.

I fell to wondering, instead, how we should persuade Professor Moriarty to comply with our bizarre request. Surely we will never induce the timid tutor to surrender his post and leave for the Continent all at once. He will demur; worse, he will whine. I turned to my companion with the object of communicating my misgivings, but he was craning his head out of the window.

"Stop here, cabbie," he directed quietly, though we were still some distance from our destination.

"If the professor was not exaggerating," Mycroft explained, forcing his bulk out of the cab, "we must be on our guard. It is essential that we talk with him, but it would not do to reveal our visit to Sherlock, should he have chosen this night to stand vigil."

I nodded and told the driver to wait for us where he stood, no matter how long it took. I pressed a shilling into his palm to ensure that he did so, and promised him yet another when we returned. Then Mycroft and I set off quietly down the deserted streets for the professor's residence.

Munro Road was in an undistinguished neighbourhood of two-storey dwellings with stucco fronts and unbecoming little gardens. At the end of the street I saw white smoke rising into the night air and clutched my portly companion by the sleeve. He looked in the direction I indicated and nodded. Together we stepped into the shadows of the nearest dwelling.

Standing beneath the only lamp on the street, Sherlock Holmes was smoking his pipe.

Edging our way closer in the shadows and crouching there, we quickly perceived that the situation was an impossible one. As long as Holmes was planted squarely opposite the professor's front door, we could not hope to enter unobserved except by a diversion; what that diversion might be we neither of us could imagine. In low whispers we held a brief consultation. The strategy of retreating to the street behind the house and entering through the back door was raised, but several arguments militated against such a ruse. There would certainly be a fence to climb, and Mycroft was obviously incapable of such gymnastics though they would not be beyond me. Even if he did master the fence, and even allowing for us to calculate the correct house in the darkness, there was still the locked back door to contend with; the inevitable commotion that followed our entry would unavoidably attract Holmes's attention.

Unexpectedly the problem was solved for us. Looking back again at the figure of my friend standing in the yellow glare of the lamp, I saw him knock the ashes from his pipe against the heel of his boot and saunter down the other end of the street.

"He's leaving!" I exclaimed in an undertone.

"Let us hope he does not intend coming back to pursue his watch," Mycroft muttered, gasping for breath as he rose and endeavoured to dust off his knees. His girth would not allow his hands to reach them. "Quickly, now," he said, giving up the effort, "we must accomplish our errand without further delay."

He struck off in the direction of the house. I stood still, watching the now distant figure of my friend in the darkness; it seemed to me that his very back—straight and narrow in his Inverness— looked lonely and forlorn.

"Watson, come on!" Mycroft hissed, and I followed him.

Rousing the inmates proved simpler than we expected; Professor Moriarty was up, his attempts at sleep having been poisoned—not for the first time —by the knowledge that Holmes was standing beneath his window.

He must have seen us approaching, for the door was opened before Mycroft's hand had reached the knocker. Moriarty, in night-shirt, cap, and faded red dressing gown, peered at us with near-sighted, sleep-hungry eyes.

"Dr. Watson?"

"Yes, and this is Mr. Mycroft Holmes. May we come in?"

"Master Mycroft!" he ejaculated in startled surprise. "Why—"

"Time is of the essence," Mycroft interrupted, smoothly reassuring. "We wish to help you as well as my brother."

"Yes, yes, of course," Moriarty agreed hastily. "Please follow me quietly. My landlady and the maids are asleep. It would not do to wake them."

When we had entered, Moriarty gently closed the door and shot the bolt.

"This way." He picked up the lamp he had deposited on the hall table and led us up the stairs into his rooms. They were reminiscent of his dressing gown—complete, but slightly worn.

"Pray do not turn up the gas," Mycroft requested, seeing that the professor was about to do so. "My brother may return, and it is essential that he not notice any change in your window."

Moriarty nodded and sat down, signing to us with a distracted wave of his hand to follow suit.

"What is to be done?" he asked desperately, for there was that in our grave faces that gave him cause to feel the matter was at least as serious as he had supposed.

"We would appreciate it very much if you would depart for Vienna in the morning," Mycroft began.

5

A Journey Through the Fog

It is not necessary to relate here what inducements we offered that night to the unfortunate mathematics instructor—what bribes, what threats, what teasings and cajolings we employed to make him serve our turn. I had not supposed Mycroft Holmes possessed such eloquence as he displayed on that bizarre occasion. Moriarty protested at first, darting little ferret-like glances from one to the other of us, his blue eyes pale in the light of the single turned-down lamp. But Mycroft convinced him. I did not know then what power the bulky giant held over the little scarecrow, but it was to Mycroft he deferred. Finally, on our promising to pay his way in the business, he at last assented, reminding us fervently what explanations we must make to Headmaster Price-Jones so that his position at the Roylott School should not be forfeit by absence.

Our bargain concluded, I went to the window and, standing carefully behind the curtain, peered down and into the street. Holmes was nowhere in sight. Signifying as much to his brother, the two of us left as we had come and returned to our cab.

On our journey back I again resisted the temptation to question Mycroft about the Holmes family's past. The temptation was even stronger than it had been to discover their secret; it was evident to me the professor had yielded to Mycroft's outrageous request because of some hold the latter had over him, a hold so powerful there was no need to even mention it. The argument, I realized in retrospect, had been conducted more for my benefit than theirs, the outcome apparently assured from the outset.

Yet resist the temptation I did, and this was not so difficult as it sounds, for I fell asleep on my side of the hansom and did not awaken until the vehicle had stopped before my door and Mycroft nudged me gently into consciousness. Quietly we said good night.

"It's all up to Sherlock now," said he.

"I wonder if we've not made it too hard for him." It was hard to keep from yawning.

Within the cab, Mycroft chuckled.

"I think not. From what you've said, his mind is the same instrument it ever was; only its emphases have been perverted. Moriarty is his man and he'll find the way to him, I think we need not concern ourselves about that. The rest is up to your doctor friend. Good night, Watson." With this, he jabbed his stick lightly on the ceiling and the hansom rattled away into the low crepuscular fog.

I must somehow have made my way to bed, but the next thing I recall is my wife standing over me and anxiously examining my face.

"Are you well, dearest?" She placed a solicitous hand on my brow as though wondering if I were feverish. I answered that I was tired but otherwise quite hale, and sat up.

"What's this?" I cried in surprise, seeing a

covered tray behind her, sitting on a chair by the door. "Breakfast in bed? I tell you I am—"

"Premonition tells me you just have time to eat it," said she unhappily, placing the tray before me.

I was about to ask her what she meant when I saw the yellow envelope lying beside the sugar.

Glancing uncertainly at my wife, who encouraged me with a brave face, I seized the envelope and opened it.

CAN YOUR PRACTISE SPARE YOU FOR A FEW DAYS? (it ran)
THE GAME IS AFOOT AND YOUR
ASSISTANCE WOULD PROVE INVALUABLE.
BRING TOBY TO ONE ONE FOUR MUNRO ROAD
HAMMERSMITH.
TAKE PRECAUTIONS.
HOLMES

Toby!

I looked up at my wife.

"It has begun," she said quietly.

"Yes." I tried to keep the thrill from my voice. The chase was on, and what would be the outcome of it time alone would tell.

I raced through my breakfast and dressing, all thought of weariness gone as my wife hurriedly packed a bag. Being married to an old army man and the daughter of another had made her a prompt and efficient packer. By the time I was ready to leave, so was my bag, except that when she was not looking I slipped my old service revolver into it. This was what Holmes had meant by TAKE PRECAUTIONS, and, though I knew I should not need it, it would be unwise to let him discover I had ignored his instructions—and equally unwise to reveal to my wife that I had followed them. I kissed her before departing, and reminded her to speak to Cullingworth about my patients.

Next I was ordered to fetch Toby and meet Holmes at the professor's home, and this I set out to do.

The street was invisible. Fog, which had gathered at my ankles some hours before, now settled still about me, much higher than my head. It was no great matter to determine its density. It was inpenetrable. All about me was a wall of sulphurous yellow smoke, stinging to the eye and noxious to the lungs. London, in a matter of hours, had been transformed into a creepy dream-world where sound replaced sight.

From different quarters my ears were assailed by horses' hoofs striking upon the cobbled street and by street vendors' cries as they hawked their wares before invisible buildings. Somewhere in the gloom an organ grinder cranked out a sinister arrangement of "Poor Little Buttercup" to add to the eerieness.

Here and there, as I edged towards the corner, using my stick to feel the way, and seeing people only the moment before it became necessary to sidestep them, I was dimly able to perceive bright glowing spots in the otherwise uniform haze of yellow. It might have taken a stranger some moments to divine that these were the street-lamps, allowed to burn in the daylight for all the good they did. I, of course, knew them at once.

It must be understood that these terrible and lethal fogs were a routine occurrence in the London where I spent my younger days. Yet even for that age, the fog through which I walked on that particular day was of extravagant dimensions.

When at last I found a cab, progress was painfully slow towards number three Pinchin Lane, Lambeth. I peered out of the window into the jaundiced void and occasionally made out some key landmark which assured me we were yet headed in the right direction. Hanover Square, Grosvenor Square, Whitehall, Westminster, and finally Westminster Bridge were shrouded stages along the way to that uninviting alley where dwelt Mr. Sherman, the naturalist, whose remarkable dog, Toby, had so often assisted Holmes in the course of his investigations.

If Toby had possessed a pedigree one would have called him a bloodhound. So far from his being a bloodhound, however, it was impossible to determine—even by Mr. Sherman, whom I had sounded once on the subject—just what Toby was. Mr. Sherman hazarded a guess of half spaniel, half lurcher, but I was not convinced. His brown and white colouring, his lopping ears, and his awkward waddle were enough to confuse me utterly regarding his antecedents.

Moreover, at some stage of his life a disease had carried off a quantity of his hair. His resultant appearance was unprepossessing to a degree. Still, Toby was a friendly and affectionate animal, and had no cause to feel inferior to the rest of the world's canines, no matter how well born. His nose was his pedigree. So far as I can determine, he never had a rival where his olfactory sense was involved. Readers may recall Toby's remarkable powers from my account of them in "The Sign of the Four," in which he was materially responsible for the discovery of the notorious Jonathan Small and his Horrible Companion. He traced them halfway across London with only a bit of creosote on the bare feet of the latter to guide him. True, he once brought us to an unexpected dead-end at a creosote barrel, but that was only because the fugitives' path had intersected that of the barrel. The dog cannot be blamed for confusing two identical scents. In fact, when Holmes and I led Toby to retrace his steps, he acknowledged the error and started forth in the correct direction with the result I have elsewhere described.

In my wildest flights of fancy I could never have guessed to what heights of genius Toby would shortly rise.

At length, from the sounds of animals squawking and crying within I knew we had arrived and I told the driver to wait. This he was not loath to do. Travel under these conditions was hazardous as well as frightening.

Stepping down, I looked about for the rows of dismal houses I knew fronted both sides of the lane, but they were not there. Only the grunts and cries of Sherman's collection led me to his door.

I knocked loudly and called out besides, for the sounds within were raucous in the extreme, as though the menagerie itself was disturbed by the awful blanket of soot and mist that deprived them of the familiar sun. But it occurred to me that they were not very often likely to be silent, and I wondered what effect this constant cacophony produced in their owner.

I had met Sherman several times when Holmes's business had brought me round for Toby. Though he had threatened me on the first occasion with a viper, that was done before he realized I was a friend of Holmes's. Upon learning that I was, he had thrown open the door and made me welcome ever since. He explained his initial hostility by informing me that he was always being "guyed at" by the children in the vicinity. It was now more than a year since I had visited him last. On that previous occasion Holmes wished to employ Toby in order to trace an orangoutan through the sewers of Marseilles. It was a case which, though I omitted to set down, was not devoid of what he deprecatingly referred to as "features of interest." As I recall, at its conclusion the Polish government recognized his services on their behalf by presenting him with the Order of St. Stanislaus, second class.*

After continual pounding and hallooing, the door at length was opened.

"All right now, you little—" The squinting eyes of the naturalist made out my form over the rims of his spectacles. "Why, Dr. Watson! I beg your pardon, I'm sure! Come in, come in. I thought it was those rapscallions playing one of their jokes in this damned fog. How ever did you find the way? Come in!"

He was holding a monkey in his arms and I was obliged to step over what I knew to be a toothless badger. The zoo suddenly fell silent as though I had cast a spell upon them. Except for the subdued cooing of a pair of grey pigeons seated together on a shelf and the squeal of a pig somewhere in a back room, the naturalist's abode was plunged into abrupt silence. In the stillness I could hear the Thames lapping at the pilings of the house. Outside the window the cry of gulls could faintly be distinguished as they swirled about aimlessly in the gloom.

---

* It is a frustrating pity that Watson did not set down the case. As it is, the Polish government's reward to Holmes for tracking an orangoutan through the sewers of Marseilles must join the number of tantalizing references the doctor makes to other cases he never saw fit to chronicle. We may infer (from the reward mentioned) that the case was brought to a successful conclusion; but *how* successful? If Holmes had succeeded entirely, might not the Polish government have awarded him the Order *first* class?

Sherman gently swept a one-eyed old tom off a ladder-backed rocker and offered the chair to me. Though I had no intention of remaining long, I sat down. Something about the man suggested a longing for human companionship, and it made me loath to dash in and out, though I knew that any delay here, coupled with the difficulties of the journey yet to be made to Hammersmith, could very well affect Toby's ability to perform at his best.

"You'll be wanting Toby, then, Doctor?" he enquired, unhooking the monkey's affectionate arm from about his neck and setting the creature down on top of a covered bird-cage. "Just a minute, then, and I'll fetch him. You've no time for a cup of tea?" he added with a rising inflection.

"I'm afraid not."

"No, I thought not." He sighed and went out through the side door to the kennels. A barking and yipping from that direction told me that his dogs were glad to see him. I discerned Toby's yelp in the midst of the din.

Sherman returned almost instantly with the animal, leaving the others howling dismally, his presence no doubt having evoked in them a similar desire to be loosed from their cages. Toby knew me and rushed forth, straining at his lead and wagging his stringy tail with ferocious energy and good will. I responded by presenting him with a lump of sugar, brought for the purpose—a regular feature of our reunions. As usual, I offered to pay Sherman in advance, and, in accordance with his own way of doing things—at least where Sherlock Holmes was concerned—he refused.

"You keep him long as you need him," he insisted as he escorted me to the door, pushing a chicken aside on the way. "We'll settle it up later. Good-bye, Toby! Here's a good doggy! Give my best to Mr. Sherlock!" he called out to me as I, with Toby in tow, stumbled towards the cab.

I called back that I would, and hailed the cabbie, who, by shouting, informed me where I had left him. Following his voice, we found the cab and climbed in. I gave the address Holmes had quoted in his telegram (and which I had visited myself the night before), and we hesitantly plunged into the round of blind traffic that was feeling its way through London.

We rediscovered Westminster Bridge, got over it—narrowly avoiding a collision with a Watney's wagon—and then headed due west towards Hammersmith. The only recognizable point along our way was Gloucester Road Station.

Turning at length into deserted Munro Road, we made for the faint glow of the sole lamp on the street, and there stopped.

"We're 'ere!" the driver announced, with as much relief as surprise in his tone, and I got out to scan the vicinity for any sign of Holmes. The place was deadly still, and my voice, when I called out his name, echoed strangely against the impenetrable mist.

I stood for a moment, perplexed, and was on the point of making my way to the professor's house—which I knew lay somewhere behind me— when I distinguished a tap-tap-tap on the pavement, somewhere to my right.

"Hullo?"

There was no answer, only the same not-quite-rhythmic tapping of a stick on the pavement. Toby reacted as I did to the sound, and let forth a little whine of unease.

The tap-tap-tapping came on.

"Hullo!" I repeated insistently. "Who is that?"

"Maxwellton braes are bonnie!" a high-pitched

tenor suddenly sang out of the mist, *"Where early fa's the dew, And it's there that Annie Laurie gie'd me her promise true—and airly fathers lie—but fur bonnie Annie Laurie, I'd lay me doun and die!"*

I stood motionless, transfixed, as the singer and the song came on, the hairs rising on the hackles of my neck at the sheer horror of it—a lonely, fog-bound London street, for all practical purposes lost to time and mind—and the piping treble of the mysterious singer ignoring my attempts to communicate.

Slowly, with shuffling gait, he drew into view, aureoled by the street lamp—a ragged minstrel with shabby, open leather waistcoat, older leather breeches, and boots held together by their laces. His white hair grew sparsely on the sides of his face, and on his head he wore a leather cap with its shovel peak turned round, all of which proclaimed to me his former association with the coal industry. I say former, for over his eyes he wore the dark-tinted spectacles of the blind.

I continued to stare in horror as this apparition drew still nearer and concluded his song. The silence hung in the air between us.

"Alms? Alms for the blind?" he intoned abruptly, and swept his hat off, holding it crown downwards before me. I fumbled in my pocket for change.

"Why didn't you answer when I called out?" I demanded of him somewhat irritably, for I was now ashamed of the impulse to which I had almost yielded, to get to my bag on the floor of the cab and fetch the revolver. I was the more irritated, perceiving how foolish such an action would have been; this blind singer held no terror for me and surely harbored no malice, either.

"I didn't like to stop the song," he answered, as if that were obvious. His accent was faintly Irish.

"When I stop the song they doesn't pay me," he explained, and shook the hat slightly before me. I dropped a few pennies into it. "Thank-ee, sir."

"But good heavens, man, how can you ply your trade in this situation?"

"Sitcheyation, sir? What sitcheyation's that?"

"Why, this blasted fog!" I retorted with energy. "You can't see your hand before your—" I stopped, suddenly remembering. The minstrel only let out a breath in exclamation.

"Oh, is *that* what's doin' it? I wondered why it was all so strange today. I don' believe I've took in a shillin' all mornin'. Fog, is it? Must be a regular corker if I haven't 'ad a shillin' on account of it. Well!"

He sighed again and appeared to look about him, a ghastly exercise in view of his deficiency.

"Do you need any help?" I enquired.

"No, no—bless you, sir, for offerin', but I don't. Why, it's all the same to me, in't? All the same to me. Thank-ee, gov'nor." And with this he scooped out the money I had placed in his hat and deposited it in his pocket. I bade him farewell and he shuffled off, using his stick before him to feel his path—no different from any ordinary man in the midst of this cursed fog—except that he was singing again, his voice dying away as he disappeared from view and was swallowed up by folds of smoke.

I looked round again and shouted once more: "*Holmes!*"

"No need to shout, Watson. I'm right here," said a familiar voice at my elbow. I jerked round and found myself nose to nose with the blind singer.

6

Toby Surpasses Himself

"Holmes!"

He laughed, tore off the false hair, and peeled away the equally false eyebrows and warts on the singer's chin. Next he removed the dark-tinted spectacles, and in place of the minstrel's dead eyes, I was treated to the sight of Holmes's twinkling ones, alight with silent mirth.

"Forgive me, my dear fellow. You know I can never resist a touch of the dramatic and the setting was so perfect that I succumbed to temptation."

It took some moments to reassure the terrified cabbie, whom the entire episode had reduced to near insensibility, but Holmes succeeded at last in calming him.

"But why the disguise?" I pursued, as he bent down to pet the dog, who, now close enough to sniff him, was happily wagging its tail and licking the paint from his cheeks. He looked up at me sharply.

"He has bolted, Watson."

"Bolted? Who has bolted?"

"The professor." Holmes spoke with an exasperated air as he stood up. "That is his house behind you in the fog. I was keeping watch on the residence myself, last night (usually I have paid Wiggins * to do it), and all was normal until midnight. It was raw and damp, and I went to the public house down the road for some brandy to warm my insides. While I was gone, two men came to see him. What they said I have no way of knowing, but I don't doubt that they were spies in his pay, come to tell him of my nets closing upon him. When I returned they had gone, and all was as I had left it. Then, this morning at eleven, I received a wire from Wiggins. Sometime between the time I left and he assumed my place, the professor departed. How or where we have yet to discover. I came here as you saw me lest his friends should lie in ambush."

I listened, trying to maintain an impassive expression and to ask the appropriate questions.

"Two men, you say?"

"Yes. One was tall and quite heavy—fourteen stone, at least—this damp ground is very effective for registering impressions. He wore large boots with a curved toe and square heel, worn towards the instep on each foot. Men that large and heavy often stand with their toes out, which accounts for this phenomenon. He was decisive, and, I should judge, the leader of the two."

"And the other?" I tried to keep from swallowing conspicuously.

"Ah, the other," Holmes sighed ruminatively and looked about at the stillness. "There are features of interest about him. He was somewhat shorter and

---

* Wiggins. An enterprising street Arab, who, for a time, directed the movements of Sherlock Holmes's "unofficial detective force" of gutter urchins, "the Baker Street Regulars."

not nearly so heavy as his companion; less than six feet, I would say, and he walked with a slight limp, not unlike yours, Watson, in his left leg. He lagged behind on one occasion and had to be called forward by the other when he approached the house. This is to be inferred from the fact that only his toe prints are visible as he went in that direction. He was running to catch up, the increased length of his stride tells me, and not being stealthy, for such a manoeuvre had not occurred to his companion. They came forward to the house, met with the professor, and took their leave. I could tell you more about them except this wretched fog has precluded my seeing the total picture of their activities. Fortunately I took precautions so that I may lay my hands on them, should that be necessary. As you know, however, it is not my habit to go after the small fish while the big ones are at large. *Mind the vanilla extract!*" he yelled suddenly, and pulled me backward from the two paces or so I had taken in the direction of the house. "You might have fallen in," he gasped, holding on to me to regain his balance. Now I was certain he was completely mad, beyond help.

"Vanilla extract?" I spoke as calmly as I could.

"Don't worry, my dear fellow, I have not lost my wits," he chuckled, releasing the lapels of my ulster. "I said I had taken precautions which would enable me to trace any or all of these men. Pay off the cab and I will explain."

Feeling very ill at ease, I stumbled back towards the cab, took my bag from its recesses, and settled with the driver. He seemed relieved to go, no doubt having judged the dangers of the fog slight compared to the hazards of life in Munro Road. The cab creaked slowly into oblivion and I returned to where my companion stood waiting. Taking me by the arm and holding Toby's lead, Holmes guided us towards the house, which, though still invisible, I was now able to sense in the nearby vicinity.

"Look down here and breathe deeply," he instructed. I squatted down and inhaled as directed, and almost at once my nostrils were assailed by the saccharine odor of vanilla extract.

"What in the world——?" I began.

"It's better than creosote, if one can arrange it," he responded, allowing Toby to smell it as well, "for it isn't sticky, which might warn the wearer that something was adhering to the soles of his boots. Its other advantage is its uniqueness. It is powerful and long-lasting, and I very much doubt that Toby will be confused by anything remotely similar—unless, of course, the trail leads us through a kitchen. Go on, smell it, boy, smell it!" he encouraged the dog, which dutifully sniffed at the large puddle of the stuff next to the kerb.

"I poured this here before I left last night," Holmes went on, continuing to remove the trappings of his disguise. "They all trod in it—Moriarty, his two accomplices, and the wheel of the cab that took him away some hours ago."

I thanked my stars that I had put on a different pair of boots this morning, and rose to my feet.

"And now?"

"And now Toby will follow the wheel of the cab. At some point he will exhibit uncertainty and we will look for the trail to continue on foot. Are you ready?"

"Are we not too late?"

"I think not. The fog that delayed your arrival no doubt interfered with his escape as well. Come on, boy!"

He jerked Toby slightly away from the puddle of vanilla extract and we were off. The scent was evidently a powerful one. Disregarding the visual handicap imposed on us by the fog, the dog went at a sharp pace, barely allowing himself to be held in check while Holmes retrieved his own satchel, a red carpet-bag, from the shrubbery on the opposite side of the road. For the most part we travelled in silence, doing our best to keep up with the animal, whose sharp tugs on the lead and enthusiastic yelps gave us to understand that not even the noxious fumes of sulphur in the air were affecting his powers.

Holmes appeared calm and collected, very much in possession of his faculties, and I was forced to wonder if I had not made some incredible error. Perhaps Moriarty *had* duped Mycroft as well as myself, and was in fact the centre of terrible evil. I put the thought out of my mind as one I could not afford at this time, and limped along as best I could in the wake of Holmes and the dog. This kind of weather was especially painful to my wound, and as a rule I did not walk in it. At one point I took out my pipe, but Holmes held up a warning hand.

"The dog has the fog to contend with already," he advised. "Let us not add to his obstacles."

I nodded and we went on, winding through streets we could not see, and dodging traffic, for we were obliged to use the centre of the road as the cab had done before us.

At one point we passed the Gloucester Road Station on our left, and I heard clearly train whistles hooting in the mists, like blind sows trying to find their litters. Still the dog pulled us on, with no apparent lapse of energy.

"I may write a monograph on it," * Holmes said, referring to the vanilla extract. "Its properties for this kind of work are ideal, as you can see. Our guide does not hesitate at all. Even through mud and water he knows his way."

I mumbled something or other in agreement and breathed again an inward sigh of relief that I had changed my footwear, else the sweet substance had led that exemplary canine to me before we had travelled two yards. The game would have been up before it had started.

As it was, I was hard-pressed to maintain the cur's pace. I could not see where we were, and the sounds of the city blurred in my ears as they succeeded one another with bewildering rapidity. My leg had begun to throb in earnest and I was on the point of saying so when Holmes stopped short and plucked me by the coat.

"What is it?" said I, gasping for breath.

"Listen."

I obeyed, trying to hear above the reverberations of my own heart. There were horses, the creakings of harness and tackle, the cries of cabbies, and the whistles of trains again.

"Victoria," Holmes said quietly.

It was indeed the great railway terminus, as we could now perceive.

"Precisely what I foresaw," Holmes murmured next to me. "You have your bag with you? That is fortunate."

Did I detect a sarcastic inflection in his tone?

---

* Holmes had in fact already written a monograph, "On the Tracing of Footsteps," a pioneer work on the subject and the first to advocate the use of plaster of Paris in taking impressions. He was the author of several privately printed articles on similar topics as well as his masterful essay "On the Polyphonic Motets of Lassus," said by experts to be the last word on the subject.

"Your wire said 'a few days,' " I reminded him.

He gave no sign of having heard, but plunged forward behind Toby, who was making a straight line for the cab stands. He sniffed in the ground next to where several of them stood idle, the horses' mouths covered with feedbags, and then suddenly made as if to dash away from the station.

"No, no," Holmes told him gently but firmly. "We are through with the cab, Toby. Show us where its passenger went."

With this, he led the animal around to the other side of the cabs and there, after a moment of hesitation, the animal's confusion was resolved. With a fresh yelp, he darted off towards the terminus itself.

Inside the crowded station—the more crowded because of the delays occasioned by the inclement weather—Toby dived through knots of stranded and irritated passengers, sometimes spilling over a portmanteau that lay in his path, till he arrived at the platform of the Continental Express. There he stopped dead before the empty tracks as Gloucester stopped at the edge of his cliff. The vanilla extract ended here. I looked at Holmes, who smiled and shot up his brows.

"So," said he, quietly.

"What now?" I enquired.

"Let us find out how long it has been since the Express has gone and how long it will be before it goes again."

"And the dog?"

"Oh, we will take him with us. I do not think we have exhausted his usefulness quite yet."

"Of course Toby is not the only method by which I might have traced Professor Moriarty," Holmes said, later, as our train emerged from the fog some twenty miles outside London on its way to Dover. "There were at least three alternatives, any one of which would have served my turn. Without vanilla extract," he added, smiling.

The clean air brought a lift to my spirits as well as to my congested lungs. Southeast of London the day was yet cloudy and rainy, but at least one could see, and the fact that I had Holmes well and truly on his way made up for any discomforts.

My companion fell into a kind of uneasy doze and awoke thirty minutes later with a start, peering at me strangely. He stood up suddenly, holding on to the overhead luggage racks for support.

"Excuse me for a moment, my dear fellow," he said in strained tones, and with another awkward glance he pulled down his red carpet-bag. He had, in the interval before our train departed from Victoria, used the facilities there to remove the last vestiges of his disguise and replace them with his normal attire, carried in the bag. I knew, therefore, where he was about to go, what he was about to do, and why he was about to do it. I choked back any remonstrance, however. This, after all, was why I was taking him to Austria. Yes, taking him, though he knew it not.

Toby raised his head from its sleeping posture as Holmes slid past us out of the compartment. I patted him and he lay still again.

Holmes returned some ten minutes later and silently replaced the carpet-bag on its rack. He sat down without a word or indeed a glance at me, and pretended to be utterly absorbed in a pocket edition of Montaigne's essays. I fell to gazing out at the rolling countryside, lightly swathed in glistening damp, the cattle standing with their backs to the wind.

The train pulled into its rendezvous with the

boat at Dover. We three disembarked briefly and stretched our legs on the platform, Holmes having provided Toby with a reminder of the vanilla extract by allowing him to catch a whiff from a small bottle of the stuff in his bag. Once on the platform, under the guise of allowing the dog to go about his business (which, indeed, he did with alacrity), we strode up and down in an effort to determine if the professor had left the train he was on when it, too, had stopped here. I, of course, knew he had not, but, as Toby came to the same conclusion, there was no need for me to say so.

"And, as the train we are taking makes only those stops that all the Continental Expresses make, we are not missing any opportunities the professor had to leave it," Holmes reasoned, and we thereupon crossed the Channel.

Using the same procedure in Calais—with the same results—we continued on our way to Paris, arriving in the middle of the night. The Gare du Nord was almost deserted at that hour and we had no difficulty in following the vanilla extract footsteps to the platform whence originated the Vienna Express.

Holmes frowned as he read the sign.

"Why on earth Vienna?" he mused.

"Perhaps he got off somewhere along the way. There appear to be plenty of stops to accommodate him. I hope Toby is infallible," I added.

Holmes smiled grimly.

"If he is not, we are a great deal worse off than when he took a wrong turning and went in search of a creosote barrel," he admitted. "But I place my faith in vanilla extract. I have conducted experiments—ah, well, if it proves false, Watson, this is one case your readers will be amused instead of amazed to read."

I did not tell him it was a case it had never occurred to me to set down.

"Vienna will replace Norbury in the lexicon of my failures," he laughed, going off to see when the next express was scheduled to depart and also to ascertain that it always left from the same platform, which, as it developed, it did.

"When the dog cannot detect the scent," Holmes reasoned as we rattled across France in the pre-dawn hours, "he will stop. As he has not stopped, I think it is safe to assume that he has not lost it. As the odor is not a common one—certainly out-of-doors—we may also infer that it is the same scent he is following and not a barrel of the substance which has crossed his path."

I nodded drowsily, trying to keep my eyes on the yellow-backed novel I had purchased in Paris, but sleep shortly overcame me.

When I awoke it was almost noon. I was covered by Holmes's hound's-tooth travelling cloak, with my legs propped up on the seat. My companion sat across from me as I had left him, staring out the window and smoking his pipe.

"Did you sleep well?" he asked, turning to me after a moment with a smile.

Aside from the crick in my neck, I answered that I had, thanking him for the loan of his cloak. I then ventured to enquire about our progress.

"We stopped twice," he informed me. "Once at the Swiss border and once at Geneva, for the better part of an hour. If Toby is to be believed, Moriarty did not leave the train."

Toby, I had cause to know, was retaining his character for infallibility. I rose, went to the washroom and shaved, and then accompanied Holmes to the dining car. There was some little fuss made about the dog, as there had been at every border, but Holmes solved this dilemma by entrusting Toby to the care of a steward, giving him some change he had converted in Paris, and asking the man to see if he could find some scraps for him from the cook's leavings. Then we settled down to luncheon, though it disturbed me to see Holmes's slight appetite was of the slightest. I again refrained from comment, however, and the day wore on. Berne succeeded Geneva and Zurich Berne. The ritual of the platform walk was repeated on the occasion of each stop, and, as it yielded only negative results, Holmes and I would return to our compartment with frowns of puzzlement on our faces. Holmes would reiterate his logic in the matter, which, I would repeat, appeared sound enough to me.

After Zurich came the German border, then Munich and Salzburg. And still there was no trace of vanilla odor on any of the train platforms.

I stared out of the window all afternoon and into the twilight, mesmerized by the scenery—so different from that at home—with its little fairy-tale cottages and quaintly dressed natives in their peaked caps, dirndls and lederhosen. The weather was sunny and gave promise of warmth. I wondered that the snow on the spectacular mountains above our route did not melt in such a climate, and said as much to Holmes.

"Oh, but it does," he replied, squinting out the window at the white-clad peaks. "And then they have avalanches."

This was not a pleasant thought, but it was impossible not to dwell upon it once it had been articulated. Were not avalanches often precipitated by sound—and were we not making a fearful racket as we plunged through these delicate structures? How if our reckless thundering should produce the tremor that would bury us?

"You are right, Watson. It is a humbling thought."

I looked at my companion who was in the act of shaking out a vesta. There was no need to ask him how he had divined my thoughts. I could easily follow the chain of reasoning involved.

"Yes, look at it." He followed my gaze upward. "How puny our actions seem when contrasted with those of Nature, do they not?" he went on with a melancholy air. "A dozen geniuses could be on this train—each one possessing some tremendous secret whose service to mankind would prove invaluable—and yet, with a flick of the Creator's little finger those distant peaks would be pushed on top of us and where would mankind be then, eh, Watson? I ask you: where does it all lead?"

He appeared to be in one of those depressions I had seen overpower him before. More surely than if he were being buried by the snow and ice he spoke of, he was hurtling downwards inside his soul and there was nothing I could do to stop him.

"Other geniuses would no doubt be born," I replied lamely.

"Ah, Watson," said he, shaking his head from side to side. "Good old Watson. You are the one fixed point in this universe of avalanches!"

I looked at him and beheld tears glistening in his eyes.

"Excuse me." He rose abruptly and took the carpet-bag with him. For once I was grateful. The drug would restore his spirits, and until I had delivered him to the care of the knowledgeable Viennese physician, I was, ironically, dependent upon it.

Shortly after Holmes returned, a tall, very red-headed Englishman opened the door of our compartment and asked, in a distracted mumble, if he might share it with us as far as Linz. He had got on the train at Salzburg, but it had filled up while he was in the dining car. Holmes urged him to be seated, with a languid wave of his hand, and appeared to show no further interest in the man. I was left to attempt a desultory conversation, which, for his part, the new arrival conducted in vague monosyllables.

"I've been for a ramble in the Tyrol," he said in answer to a question of mine, and Holmes opened his eyes.

"In the Tyrol? Surely not," said he. "Doesn't the label on your baggage state that you have just returned from Ruritania?"

The handsome Englishman turned almost as pale as Holmes. He got to his feet, repossessed his bags and, mumbling apologies, said he was going to have a drink.

"What a pity," I remarked after he had gone, "I should have liked to ask him about the coronation."

"Mr. Rassendyll did not wish to discuss it," Holmes declared, "else he would have left his gear with us instead of taking it to the club car. This way he has no reason to return."

"What an extraordinary head of hair! One would have instantly granted him entrance to the League,* eh, Holmes?"

"No doubt," he replied drily.

"You say his name's Rassendyll? I couldn't make out the label."

"No more could I."

"Then how in the name of all that's wonder-

---

* Watson refers here to The Red-Headed League, a bogus society that ostensibly aided and employed men with pure-red hair. In the case labelled *The Adventure of the Red-Headed League* the reader will be supplied with complete details.

ful—?" I began, but he cut me off with a brief laugh and a wave of his hand.

"I've no wish to make a mystery of the matter," said he. "I recognized him, that is all. He is the younger brother of Lord Burlesdon.† I chatted with him at a party at Lord Topham's once. Rather a ne'er-do-well," he concluded, losing interest in the subject as the drug's effects made themselves felt.

It was quite dark when the train pulled into Linz and we took Toby for his perambulation on the platform. By this time, Holmes himself was convinced that Moriarty had gone all the way to Vienna (though for what reason he still could not imagine), and, therefore, it did not surprise him when the dog failed to react to any olfactory stimuli in the station.

We reboarded the train and slept all the way to Vienna, which we reached in the early hours of the morning.

Again we went through the process of shaving and donning clean linen, but this time we were conscious of suppressed excitement, of prolonging the dramatic moment when Toby would step out on the platform and see if any vanilla extract was to be detected.

Finally the time had come. Crossing our fingers for luck, Holmes and I stepped out of the train, carrying our bags and holding Toby's lead. We

---

† Here is one of the great accidental meetings in recent English history, pregnant with all sorts of irony. Watson appears to have gone to his grave without ever knowing just who the remarkable handsome red-headed fellow traveller was. As Holmes deduced, he was in fact just returned from Ruritania, and not the Tyrol. His experiences in that kingdom and an interesting eye-witness account of the coronation of King Rudolph V can be found in Mr. Rassendyll's book on the subject, *The Prisoner of Zenda,* published in 1894 under the pen-name, Anthony Hope.

walked slowly from one end of the train to the other, and had only one more car to go, but still Toby gave no sign that served as a hopeful indication. Holmes's face grew long as we approached the gate which led to the terminus.

Suddenly the dog froze in his tracks, then darted forward a foot or two along the platform, his nose plowing through the soot on the ground and his tail wagging in jubilation.

"He's found it!" we exclaimed simultaneously. He had indeed, and after setting up his own growls and whines of satisfaction, Toby turned about and started rapidly towards the gate.

He led us through that foreign railroad station as though it were Pinchin Lane, a thousand miles away. No frontiers, no barrier of language made the slightest impression on Toby or in the least interfered with his pursuit of the vanilla extract. Had the scent been strong enough—and had Professor Moriarty taken it into his head to do so—that dog would cheerfully have followed him around the globe.

As it was, he led us to the cab stand outside the terminus and stopped, looking at us with a hurt expression in his eyes that begged for forgiveness. At the same time he reproached us with being somehow responsible for matters coming to this pass. Holmes, however, was not disturbed.

"It appears he has taken a cab," he observed calmly. "Now in England, hansoms that cater to the railroad trade generally return to the station after they have delivered their fare. Let us see if Toby is interested in any of the cabs."

He was not, however. Holmes sat down next to our bags on a bench just inside the main entrance, and thought.

"Several possibilities occur to me, but I believe the simplest one, for the moment, is to stay here and let Toby examine every cab as it arrives in line at the stand." He looked up at me. "Are you hungry?"

"I breakfasted on the train while you were asleep," I replied.

"Well, I think I should enjoy a cup of tea." He rose and handed me Toby's lead. "I'll be in the buffet, should luck favour us."

He went his way and I returned to the cab stand where the drivers were suitably mystified by my behaviour. Toby and I would walk up to every new cab as it took its place in the line, and I would extend my arm encouraging him to go forward and sniff at it. Some of the drivers were amused at this ceremony, while one beefy gentleman with a face as red as a beet protested vociferously, and even with my schoolboy German I was able to comprehend his alarm: he feared Toby was about to deface the vehicle. Indeed, that once turned out to be his intention, but I managed to pull him away just in time.

A half-hour passed by in this fashion. Long before it was over, Holmes emerged, carrying both our bags, and stood watching. There was no need to speak, and after some moments he came forward and sighed.

"It won't do, Watson," he said. "Let us go to a hotel where I will make other arrangements. Cheer up, old friend. I said there were several possibilities. Cab!"

We stepped up to a new arrival, ready to get in, when suddenly Toby broke out with a bark of joy and began wagging his tail with emphasis. Holmes and I looked at each other in astonishment, then burst out laughing together.

"All things come to those who wait, Watson!" he chuckled, and went to speak with the driver.

Holmes's German was better than mine, though not by much. Aside from memorized quotations from Goethe and Schiller—no doubt also culled from schooldays and of little use to us now—his knowledge of most languages (except French, which he spoke fluently) was confined to the vocabulary of crime. He could say "murder," robbery," "forgery," "revenge," and such in a variety of tongues, and knew a few related sentences in each, but little else, besides.* In the present instance he appeared to be at a loss to describe Moriarty, but the cab-man was polite, especially when Holmes offered him some money. He had purchased a language aid at the book counter next to the buffet, and this he whipped out, thumbing frantically in an effort to enlarge his command of German. The cumbersome method bore no fruit and I was not sorry when another driver, one who had been much amused by my antics earlier, called down from his perch that he knew "some small English" and offered to help.

"Thank heavens," my companion murmured, "all I can find here is: 'The weather is most becoming, do you not think so?"

He pocketed the book and addressed himself to our interpreter.

"Tell him," Holmes said, speaking slowly and distinctly, "that we want him to take us to the place where he took another passenger within the past few hours." He proceeded to furnish our interpreter with a detailed description of Moriarty, which was then repeated in German for the benefit of the driver of the cab in which Toby had evinced such a pronounced interest.

---

* It was undoubtedly this cursory knowledge that enabled Holmes to identify the bloody writing on the wall of the Lauriston Gardens house in "A Study in Scarlet."

When this communication was but half completed the driver suddenly beamed, uttered a bellowing, "Ach, ja!" and waved us hospitably into the vehicle.

The moment we were seated, he snapped the reins and we were off through the busy, beautiful streets of the city of Johann Strauss—and also the city of Metternich, depending on your own associations. I had no idea where we were or where we were going, never having been in Vienna before. We passed through colorful squares, near imposing statues, and stared out of our windows at the interesting natives of that city who, unaware of our inquisitive presence, went about their morning's business.

I remarked above that "we" stared out of the windows; but this is only two-thirds of the truth. I stared out the window and Toby stared out the window. But for Holmes, as always on such occasions, the scenery, however quaint or dramatic, held no attractions. Contenting himself with observing the names of the streets we traversed, he lit his pipe and settled back against the cushions, his mind devoted to the business at hand.

With an abrupt mental jolt, I too recalled the business at hand. In a few moments—should nothing go amiss—Holmes and I would come face to face with the doctor on whose help I so totally depended for Holmes's recovery. What would Holmes's reaction be? Would he cooperate? Would he even admit his difficulty? Would he be grateful or infuriated that his friends had taken so enormous a liberty with him? And how would he view being duped with his own methods, hoist with his own petard?

I banished these last thoughts the moment they arose. I cared not for his gratitude, and it would scarcely surprise me if he did not display it, under the circumstances. No, the important thing, my paramount concern, was that he be cured. Let that happen and all other travail and livid rebuke might be easily borne.

The cab pulled up to a small but attractive building on a side street just off a major thoroughfare. Its name, in my preoccupation, I failed to note. The driver by various signs and gestures gave us to understand this was the destination of the gentleman we were seeking.

We got out and Holmes paid the man, after a brief consultation.

"We may have been robbed, but it was worth it," he confided in high good humour when the cab had pulled away. We turned our attention to the house itself, and Holmes rang the bell. I noticed, with relief, a small plaque which quietly proclaimed the name of the man we had come to see.

A moment later the door was opened by a pretty maid, who was only briefly startled by the presence of such a peculiar-looking dog in the company of two visitors.

Sherlock Holmes informed her of our identities and she responded at once with a smile, and an invitation, couched in broken English, to enter.

We nodded and followed her inside, finding ourselves in a small but elegant entrance hall with a white marble floor. The house was some kind of Viennese chocolate bread miniature, crammed with Dresden knick-knacks of every description. To one side, a thin black bannistered staircase led up to a charming little balcony that ran in a semi-circle over our heads.

"Please, this way—come," the maid gestured, still smiling openly, and she ushered us into a cramped study which opened off the vestibule. When we had seated ourselves, she offered to take Toby and find him something to eat. Holmes vetoed this at once, with cold formality, looking at me significantly around the shoulder of the girl, as much as to say, "What sort of meal might we expect to be given our valiant Toby under this particular roof?" But I argued that the professor would never dare any manoeuvre so precipitate.

"Oh, very well, perhaps you are right," he agreed, considering the matter while smiling icily at the grinning maid, who waited for our decision. I could see that he was tiring again and in need of an injection—or something better. I thanked the maid and handed over Toby's lead to her.

"Well, Watson, what do you make of it all?" Holmes demanded when she had gone.

"I can make nothing of it," I confessed, seeking refuge in the familiar response, instead of anticipating events. The doctor, I felt, should have the right to explain the situation in his own way.

"And yet it is obvious enough—obvious though horribly diabolical," he amended, pacing back and forth and examining the doctor's books, which, though mainly in German, were easily perceived as being of a medical character—at least on the side where I was seated.

I was on the point of asking Holmes to explain his remark when the door was opened and into the room stepped a bearded man of medium height and stooped shoulders. I took him to be in his early forties though I subsequently learned he was only thirty-five. Through his faint smile I saw an expression of infinite sadness, coupled, as it seemed to me, with infinite wisdom. His eyes were more remarkable than anything else in his face. They were not particularly large, but they were dark and deep-set, shadowed by an over-hanging brow and piercing in their intensity. He wore a dark suit with a gold chain peeping under his jacket and stretched across his waistcoat.

"Good morning, Herr Holmes," said he, in heavily accented but otherwise perfect English. "I have been expecting you and am glad that you decided to come. And you, Dr. Watson," he added, turning to me with a gracious smile and extended hand, which I shook, briefly, my eyes unable to leave Holmes's face.

"You may remove that ludicrous beard," he said in the high-pitched voice which he had displayed on the night he burst so melodramatically into my house, and used again the following day when I had visited him in his. "And kindly refrain from employing that ridiculous comic opera accent. I warn you, you'd best confess or it will go hard with you. That game is up, Professor Moriarty!"

Our host turned slowly to him, allowing for the full effect of his piercing gaze, and said, in a soft voice: "My name is Sigmund Freud."

7

Two Demonstrations

There followed a long silence. Something in the manner of the physician gave Holmes pause. Excited though he was, he controlled himself with a visible effort, and approached the man, who had quietly eased himself into a chair behind the cluttered desk. He gazed at him steadily for some moments and then sighed.

"You are not Professor Moriarty," he conceded at length. "But Moriarty was here. Where is he now?"

"At a hotel, I believe," the other answered, maintaining his steady gaze.

Holmes withdrew before it, turned, and resumed his chair with a look of inexpressible defeat.

"Well, Iscariot," he turned to me, "you have delivered me into the hands of my enemies. I trust they will recompense you for the trouble you took in their behalf." He spoke with a lassitude underlined by a calm certainty, and his words would have convinced me had I not known for a fact that he was utterly deluded.

"Holmes, this is unworthy of you!" I flushed, mortified and angered by the outrageous epithet.

"That is the pot calling the kettle black, if I am not mistaken," he retorted. "However, let us not quibble. I recognized your footprints outside the professor's home; I perceived that you brought with you a Gladstone bag, suggesting that you knew we should be going on a journey. The amount of luggage told me you knew in advance how long it would be, and I was able to see for myself that you prepared for a voyage precisely as long as the one we undertook. I only wish to know what you plan to do with me now that I am in your power."

"If you will permit me a word," Sigmund Freud interjected quietly, "I believe you are doing your friend a grave injustice. He did not bring you to see me with any intention of doing you harm." He spoke calmly, easily, and with soft assurance, despite the fact that he was speaking in a foreign tongue. Holmes refocused his attention on the man. "As for Professor Moriarty, Dr. Watson and your brother paid him a considerable sum of money to journey here in the hope that you would follow him to my door."

"And why did they do that?"

"Because they were sure it was the only way they could induce you to see me."

"And why were they so eager for that particular event?" I knew that Holmes must be badly confused but he was no longer showing it. He was not a man to err twice.

"What reason occurs to you?" the doctor countered surprisingly. "Come, I have read the accounts of your cases and just now have I seen a glimpse of your astonishing faculties. Who am I and why should your friends be so eager to have us meet?"

Holmes eyed him coldly.

"Beyond the fact that you are a brilliant Jewish physician who was born in Hungary and studied for a time in Paris, and that some radical theories of yours have alienated the respectable medical community so that you have severed your connections with various hospitals and branches of the medical fraternity—beyond the fact that you have ceased to practise medicine as a result, I can deduce little. You are married, possess a sense of honour, and enjoy playing cards and reading Shakespeare and a Russian author whose name I am unable to pronounce. I can say little besides that will be of interest to you."

Freud stared at Holmes for a moment in utter shock. Then, suddenly, he broke into a smile—and this came as another surprise to me, for it was a child-like expression of awe and pleasure.

"But this is wonderful!" he exclaimed.

"Commonplace," was the reply. "I am still awaiting an explanation for this intolerable ruse, if ruse it was. Dr. Watson may tell you that it is very dangerous for me to leave London for any length of time. It generates in the criminal classes an unhealthy excitement when my absence is discovered."

"Still," Freud insisted, smiling with fascination, "I should very much like to know how you guessed the details of my life with such uncanny accuracy."

"I never guess," Holmes corrected smoothly. "It is an appalling habit, destructive to the logical faculty." He rose, and though he tried not to show it, I suspected a thaw was creeping into his replies. Holmes could be as vain as a girl about his gifts, and there was nothing patronizing or insincere in the Viennese doctor's admiration. He now prepared to forget or ignore the danger he supposed he was in, and to enjoy his last moments to the fullest.

"A private study is an ideal place for observing facets of a man's character," he began in a familiar tone, reminiscent of an anatomy professor explicating the intricacies of a skeleton before a class. "That the study belongs to you, exclusively, is evident from the dust. Not even the maid is permitted here, else she would hardly have ventured to let matters come to this pass," and he swept a finger over some nearby bindings, accumulating soot on the tip.

"Go on," Freud requested, clearly delighted.

"Very well. Now when a man is interested in religion, and possesses a well-stocked library, he generally keeps all books on such a subject in one place. Yet your editions of the Koran, the King James Bible, the Book of Mormon, and various other works of a similar nature are separate—across the room, in fact—from your handsomely bound copy of the Talmud and a Hebrew Bible. These, therefore, do not enter into your studies merely, but constitute some special importance of their own. And what could that be, save that you are yourself of the Jewish faith? The nine-branched candelabrum on your desk confirms my interpretation. It is called a Menorah, is it not?

"Your studies in France are to be inferred from the great many medical works you possess in French, including a number by someone named Charcot. Medicine is complex enough already and not to be studied in a foreign language for one's private amusement. Then, too, the well-worn appearance of these volumes speaks plainly of the many hours you have spent poring over them. And where else should a German student read French medical texts but in France? It is a longer shot, but the particularly dog-eared appearance of those works of Charcot—whose name seems to have a contemporary ring—makes me venture to suggest that he was your own teacher; either that, or his writing had some special appeal for you, connected with the development of your own ideas. It can be taken for granted," Holmes went on with the same didactic formality, "that only a brilliant mind could penetrate the mysteries of medicine in a foreign tongue, to say nothing of concerning itself with the wide range of subject matter covered by the books in this library."

He walked about the room as if it were a laboratory and nothing more, paying us only the most cursory attention as he continued his lecture.

Freud watched, leaning back with his fingers interlaced across his waistcoat. He was unable to stop smiling.

"That you read Shakespeare is to be deduced from the fact that the book has been replaced upside-down. You can scarcely miss it here amidst the English literature, but the fact that you have not adjusted the volume suggests to my mind that you no doubt intended pulling it out again in the near future, which leads me to believe that you are fond of reading it. As for the Russian author—"

"Dostoievski," Freud prompted.

"Dostoievski . . . the lack of dust on that volume —also lacking on the Shakespeare, incidentally— proclaims your consistent interest in it. That you are a physician is obvious to me when I glance at your medical degree on the far wall. That you no longer practise medicine is evident by your presence here at home in the middle of the day, with no apparent anxiety on your part about a schedule to keep. Your separation from various societies is indicated by those spaces on the wall, clearly meant to display additional certificates. The color of the paint is there somewhat paler in small rectangles, and an outline of dust shows me where they used to be. Now, what can it be that forces a man to remove such testimonials to his success? Why, only that he has ceased to affiliate himself with those various societies, hospitals, and so forth. And why should he do this, since once he troubled himself to join them all? It is possible that he became disillusioned with one or two, but not likely that disenchantment with the lot of them set in, and all at once. Therefore I conclude that it is they who became disenchanted with you, doctor, and asked that you resign your membership in each of them. And why should they do this—and in a body, from the look of the wall? You are still living placidly enough in the same city where this has all taken place, so some position you have taken—evidently a professional one—has discredited you in their eyes and they have in response—all of them—asked you to leave. What can this position be? I have no real idea, but your library, as I noted earlier, is evidence of a far-ranging, enquiring, and brilliant mind. Therefore I take the liberty of postulating some sort of radical theory, too advanced or too shocking to gain ready acceptance in current medical thinking. Possibly the theory is connected with the work of the M. Charcot who seems to have been such an influence on you. That is not certain. Your marriage is, however. It is plainly blazoned forth on the finger of your left hand, and your Balkanized accent hints at Hungary or Moravia. I do not know that I have omitted anything of importance in my conclusions."

"You said that I possessed a sense of honour," the other reminded him.

"I am hoping that you do," Holmes replied. "I inferred it from the fact that you bothered to remove the plaques and testimonials of those societies which have ceased to recognise you. In the privacy of your own home you might have permitted them to remain and made what discreet capital out of them that you would, and no one the wiser."

"And my love of cards?"

"Ah, that is a point of greater subtlety still, but I will not insult your intelligence by describing how I came to know it. Rather, I turn to you in candour and ask that you now tell me what it is that has brought me all this way to see you. It was not merely for the sake of so elementary a demonstration."

"I asked you before," Freud said with a smile, his admiration for Holmes's abilities still evident in his face, "why *you* thought you had been tricked into coming here."

"I have no idea," Holmes responded with a touch of his earlier asperity. "If you are in trouble, say so, and I will do my best to help you, though why you should have gone about securing my presence in this fashion—"

"Then it is *you* who are not being logical," interposed the doctor gently. "As you have so ably deduced, I am in no particular difficulty—other than the professional one to which you have alluded," he amended with a brief inclination of his massive head in the direction of the absent plaques. "And, as you point out, the method used to bring you here was unorthodox in the extreme. Clearly, we did not think you would come of your own accord. Does this suggest nothing to you?"

"That I would not wish to come," Holmes responded unwillingly.

"Precisely. And why? Not because you feared we intended you harm. *I* might be your enemy; Professor Moriarty might be, as well. Even—excuse me—Dr. Watson. But is it likely your brother would be of our number? Is it likely we *all* are in league against you? For what purpose? If not to do you harm, then perhaps to do you good. Had you thought of that?"

"And what good might that be?"

"You cannot guess?"

"I never guess. I cannot think."

"No?" Freud leaned back in his chair. "Then *you* are being less than candid, Herr Holmes. For you are suffering from an abominable addiction, and you choose to wrong your friends who have combined to help you throw off its yoke rather than to admit your own culpability. You disappoint me, sir. Is this the Holmes I have read about? The man whom I have come to admire not only for his brain but for his princely chivalry, his passion for justice, his compassion for suffering? I cannot believe that you are so subjugated by the power of this drug that you do not, in your heart of hearts, acknowledge your difficulty as well as your own hypocrisy in condemning the staunch friends, who, solely out of love for you and concern for your well-being, have taken so many pains on your account."

I found that I was holding my breath. In my long acquaintance with Sherlock Holmes I had never heard anyone address him in such fashion. For a moment I feared some incredible outbreak of fury on the part of my unfortunate friend. I had underestimated him, however, as Sigmund Freud had not.

There was another long pause. Holmes sat motionless, with his head bowed. The doctor did not take his eyes off him and the room was deathly still.

"I have been guilty of these things," Holmes spoke at last, and in a voice so low it was almost impossible to catch the words. Freud leaned forward. "I make no excuse," he went on, "but as for help, you must put it out of your minds, all of you. I am in the grip of this devilish malady and it will consume me! No, don't try to reassure me; you mustn't." He held up a protesting hand, then let it fall helplessly to his side. "I have applied all my will to banishing this habit and I have not been able to do so. And if I, summoning all my resolve, cannot succeed, what chance have you? Once a man takes the first false step, his feet are set forever on the path to his destruction."

I realized, in my corner of the room, that my mouth was hanging open and my breast heaving with emotion. The silence was electric and I did not dare to break it. Dr. Freud, however, did.

"Your feet are not set inexorably on the path," he replied, leaning forward with quiet urgency, his eyes bright. "A man can turn around and leave that path to destruction, though it may require some help. The first step need not be fatal."

"It always is," groaned Holmes, in a despairing voice that wrung my heart. "No man has ever done what you describe."

"I have done it," said Sigmund Freud.

Holmes looked up slowly with an expression of vague wonder.

"You?"

Freud nodded.

"I have taken cocaine and I am free of its power. If you will allow me, I will help you to free yourself as well."

"You cannot do this." Holmes's voice was breathless. Though he protested that he did not believe, yet his tone told me how desperately he wished to hope.

"I can."

"How?"

"It will take time." The doctor stood up. "For

the duration I have arranged that you both shall remain here as my guests. Will that be agreeable to you?"

Holmes rose automatically and started forward, but then he suddenly whirled about, clapping an agonized hand to his brow.

"It's no use!" he wailed. "Even now I am overcome by this hideous compulsion!"

I half rose from my chair, with some thought of comforting him with a word of encouragement and good cheer, but stopped in my tracks, realizing the futility—the mockery, even—of such a gesture.

Dr. Freud came slowly round his desk and put a small hand gently on my friend's shoulder.

"I can stop this compulsion—for a time. Sit down, please." He motioned to the chair from which Holmes had risen, and seated himself on the edge of his desk. Holmes silently obeyed and sat waiting, his posture indicative of his misery and pessimism.

"Do you know anything of the practise of hypnotism?" Freud enquired.

"Something," Holmes returned wearily. "Do you propose to make me bark like a dog and crawl about on all fours?"

"If you will cooperate," Freud said, "if you will trust me, I can reduce your craving for a time. When next it exerts its attractions, I will hypnotize you again. In this way we shall artificially reduce your addiction until the chemistry of your body completes the process." He spoke very slowly, taking pains to penetrate and subdue the rising tide of Holmes's panic and mortification.

Holmes studied him for a length of time when he had done speaking, and then, with an abrupt shrug of his hunched shoulders, he acquiesced, with a studied insouciance.

Dr. Freud restrained himself from sighing aloud, it appeared to me, and went to the bow window, drawing the curtains, plunging the room into semidarkness. Then he returned to Holmes, who had not moved a muscle.

"Now," Freud began, pulling up a chair opposite him, "I want you to sit up straight and keep your eyes fixed on this."

And he drew from his waistcoat pocket the watch fob I had glimpsed earlier, and commenced swinging the end of it slowly back and forth.

PART 2
The
Solution

8

A Holiday in Hell

Professor Moriarty's initial reluctance to journey back to London in the company of Toby lent a touch of comic relief to an otherwise ghastly week. He took one look at the dog—when I brought him round to his hotel in the Graben that afternoon— and announced that he was a man of good-will (as evidenced by his journey to Vienna in the first place) but that there was a limit to his generosity beyond which it was impossible to trespass.

"That," he said, looking over his spectacles at Toby, who returned his gaze with an eager and willing expression of his own, "is the limit. I am a patient man—a desperate man, I grant you, but a patient one, Dr. Watson. I have not said a word about the vanilla extract that has totally ruined a new pair of boots, have I? But this is too much. I will not transport that animal back to London, no, not for Cadwallader and all his goats."

I was in no mood to trifle with him, however, and told him so. If he wished to let Toby travel with the luggage, he was at liberty to do so, but return the animal to Pinchin Lane he must. I referred obliquely to Mycroft Holmes, and Moriarty—still whining—backed down and subsided into muttered asides.

I sympathized with his complaints but was in no position to listen to them. My own nerves were frayed to the breaking point, and a reassuring telegram from my wife, saying that all was well at home, was the only comfort I could pluck for myself. It was little enough.

Sherlock Holmes's attempt to escape from the coils of the cocaine in which he was so deeply enmeshed was perhaps the most harrowing and heroic effort I have ever witnessed. In both my professional and personal experience, in both military and civilian life, I cannot recall anything to equal the sheer agony of it.

That first day, Dr. Sigmund Freud had been successful. He managed to mesmerize Holmes and put him to sleep in one of the adjoining rooms he had placed at our disposal on the second floor of his home. No sooner was Holmes stretched out on the elaborately carved bed than Freud grasped my sleeve urgently. "Quickly!" he commanded. "We must search all his possessions."

I nodded, not needing to be told what we were looking for, and the two of us began rifling Holmes's carpet-bag and also the pockets of his clothes. It went against many of my principles thus to obtrude on my friend's privacy. But we were playing for high stakes, and I hardened my heart as I bent to the task.

There was no difficulty in finding bottles of cocaine. Holmes had traveled to Vienna with enormous quantities of the drug. It was a wonder, I thought, pulling forth bottles from the recesses of the bag, that I had not heard them clinking against each other en route; but Holmes had prevented this by wrapping the bottles in the black velvet cloth whose use was normally reserved for covering his Stradivarius in its case. Without pausing to acknowledge the pain in my breast when I saw to what purpose he had adapted the cloth, I continued to retrieve the deadly vials and hand them to Dr. Freud, who had dextrously completed an inspection of the sleeping man's pockets and his Inverness travelling cloak, where he had discovered two more containers.

"I think we have them," said he.

"Don't be certain," I adjured him. "You are not dealing with an ordinary patient." He shrugged and watched as I took the stopper from a bottle and moistened the tip of my finger with the colourless liquid and then touched my tongue with it.

"Water!"

"Can it be?" Freud sampled the contents of another vial and looked over at me in astonishment. Behind us, Holmes rolled over in uneasy slumber. "Where is he hiding it, then?"

We thought desperately, not knowing when the sleeper might awaken and our troubles begin in earnest. It had to be here, somewhere. Emptying the entire contents of the carpet-bag on the luxuriant oriental rug, we perused the meagre effects Holmes had brought with him from London. His linen yielded nothing, nor did the grease-paint and other paraphernalia of his disguise. For the most part, what remained consisted of some unconverted English silver and notes, and his familiar pipes. The black briar, the oily clay, and the long cherrywood were well known to me, and offered, I knew, no place for concealment. There was, however, a large calabash I had never seen before, and, picking it up, I was surprised to find it heavier than its size warranted.

"Look at this." I removed the meerschaum top

and turned the big gourd upside down. Out fell a small bottle.

"I begin to see what you mean," the doctor admitted, "but where else can he have secreted them? There are no more pipes."

We stared at one another over the top of the empty bag, and then, in the same instant, stretched out our hands for it. Freud's thought was a moment before mine, however. He picked up the bag and hefted it, shaking his head.

"Too heavy," he muttered, passing it to me. I put my hand inside it and knocked softly on the base. It gave out a muffled, hollow retort. "A false bottom!" I exclaimed, and set about pulling it up. In a matter of moments I had peeled back the inserted board, and there, beneath it, cunningly nestled amongst crumpled agony columns from the London papers, we discovered the true cache of cocaine and the syringe, which occupied a patch of red velvet in a small black box.

Without a word we retrieved the hoard, including the bottled water, replaced the false bottom and the contents of the bag, and went downstairs together. Freud led me to a washroom on the first floor, and into the sink we poured all the liquid we had found. He pocketed the syringe and escorted me to the kitchen, where the maid, whose name was Paula, returned Toby to my charge and I left for Moriarty's hotel.

I must pause here and give some description of the city in which I found myself and in which I was destined to remain for some little time.

Vienna in 1891 was the capital of an empire in the final decades of its flowering. It was as totally unlike London at the same period as the sea is unlike the desert. London, habitually damp, foggy, ill-smelling, and populated for the most part with people who spoke one language, bore no resemblance to the sunny and decadent centre of the Hapsburg Empire. Instead of a common tongue, the natives conversed in a polyglot derived, even as they themselves were, from the four corners of the Austro-Hungarian realm. Although these various nationalities tended to restrict themselves to separate quarters of the city, their territories frequently overlapped. It was an unusual day when one did not see Slovak peddlers hawking their hand-carved wares to fashionable housewives as a squadron of Bosnian infantry marched by towards the Prater for a review of the Emperor's troops, while lemon sellers from Montenegro, knife sharpeners from Serbia, and Tyrolers, Moravians, Croats, Jews, Hungarians, Bohemians, and Magyars all went about their daily business.

The city itself appeared to grow in concentric circles with the cathedral of St. Stephen's at the hub. Here one found the fashionable and oldest quarter of the town with the Graben, its busy street of shops and cafes, to the north of which, at Bergasse 19, dwelt Dr. Freud. Slightly to the left lay the Hofburg palaces, museums, and beautifully kept parks. Just outside these the "inner city" ended. The walls that once defended the medieval Vienna had long since been torn down—at the pleasure of the Emperor—and the city spread far beyond them. Still their outline was preserved in the form of a wide boulevard that went by different names in several sections but was generally known as The Ring, and extended around the old quarter ending at the Danube Canal, due north and due east of St. Stephen's.

The city, as I have noted, had outgrown the medieval set of boundaries represented by The Ring, and in 1891 even overflowed the Gürtel—an outer boulevard—some of which was still under construction and renovation when I was there. The Gürtel, whose course unevenly paralleled that of The Ring, stood, at its southwestern extremity, about half-way between St. Stephen's cathedral and Maria Theresa's Schönbrunn palace—the Hapsburg response to Versailles.

Just north of Schönbrunn and slightly to the east, in the Fifteenth Bezirk, lay the *Bahnhof,* or railway terminus where Holmes and I had arrived in Vienna. All the way across the city to the northeast in the Second Bezirk (across the Danube Canal), was situated a much larger railway yard in the midst of a predominantly Jewish sector known as the Leopoldstadt. It was there, Dr. Freud told me, that he had lived as a child when he first came with his family to the city.

His present home was far more convenient professionally—(for Holmes was erroneous in one of his deductions: Freud was still practising medicine). It was close to the Allgemeines Krankenhaus, the great teaching hospital of Vienna, to which he had been formerly attached. He had served in the Psychiatric Department under a Dr. Theodor Meynert, a man for whom he had great admiration.

Like Freud, Meynert was a Jew, but this was by no means a surprising feature in Viennese medical circles, which, Freud informed me, were very largely composed of Jews. They appeared to dominate much of the intellectual and cultural activity in the city. I had not met many Jews and so knew little about them though I may claim, for all that, to be reasonably free of the prejudice which usually accompanies ignorance. As I was to discover, Freud was not only a brilliant man and a cultivated one, he was also a good man, and as far as I am concerned (though I disagreed with some of his theories which I found frankly shocking), these virtues of his were of more moment than his faith—about which, by the way—he was himself uncertain. Not being a religious man myself, I was unable to rouse in my bosom any particular ire or yen for dogmatic controversy with a supposed heathen.

I realize that I have digressed slightly from my description of the city and inexorably begun the resumption of my narrative, which is perhaps just as well. I did not learn about Vienna in one lump and there is no need for the reader to be confronted with a travelogue when an almanac will do. What parts and places of the city engaged my attention when I stayed there will shortly become apparent, in any event.

After leaving Toby with his unwilling chaperone, I proceeded down the Graben to the Cafe Griensteidl, which occupied an inescapably prominent location in the middle of the street. There I was to rendezvous with Dr. Freud should Holmes still be asleep.

To call the Griensteidl a cafe is to do it a gross injustice, for it did not in the least resemble what Englishmen mean by the word. Cafes in Vienna were more like London's clubs. They were the centre of intellectual and cultural exchange where a man might put in a pleasant day and never taste a drop of coffee. The Griensteidl boasted billiard tables, chess niches, newspapers, and books. Its waiters took efficient messages and set a fresh glass of water at your table every hour, whether you bought anything to eat or not. Cafes were where men met to exchange ideas, to talk, to read, or to be alone. They were a good place for one to gain weight in, for the bill of fare included the most extravagant pastries, and it was a strong-willed patron who could resist their aromatic blandishments.

Freud was at the Griensteidl (which, by the by, laid claim to being the most cultivated institution of its kind in the city), and a waiter directed me to his table. I ordered beer, and listened as he informed me that Holmes was still asleep, though it would be necessary to return to Bergasse 19 before long. We seemed, each of us, unwilling to plunge at once into the many questions and issues that needed resolution if we were to effect a cure, and it was then that Freud told me something of his background and of the present nature of his work. Cocaine, he explained, was more or less a side-line and not directly related to his present researches. He and two other physicians had become interested in the drug when they discovered its invaluable anaesthetic properties for use during eye surgery. Freud had been trained as a neuropathologist, with a background in localized diagnosis and electroprognosis—terms which were quite beyond the ken of a simple practitioner like myself.

"Yes, I have come a long way—and by a circuitous route," he smiled, "from mapping the nervous system to where I am now."

"You are an alienist?"

He shrugged.

"There is no formal designation for what I am now," he responded. "As Herr Holmes has deduced. I am interested in hysterical cases, and for the most part they come to me—referred by their families—or I go to them, privately. Where my studies are leading I cannot say with certainty, but I am learning a great deal about hysterics, and what I call neurotics."

I was about to ask him what he meant by this

last term and whether Holmes had been correct in assuming that some of his theories had been found unpalatable by the medical community, when he quietly interrupted and suggested that we return to our resident patient. As we threaded our way amongst the tables and knots of earnestly conversing artists and writers, he offered, over his shoulder, to take me along on some of his rounds so that I might see for myself the people he treated, and their symptoms. I accepted with pleasure, and we began walking through the bustling Graben, and boarded a horse-drawn streetcar that ran on rails.

"Tell me," I said, when we were seated, "do you know an English doctor named Conan Doyle?"

He pursed his lips in an effort to remember.

"Should I?" he asked at length.

"Possibly. He studied for a time in Vienna, specializing as an ophthalmologist like your colleagues—"

"Königstein and Koller?"

"Yes. Perhaps they knew him when he studied here."

"Perhaps." His noncommittal answer did not contain an offer to ask his two collaborators if they knew Doyle. Perhaps they were among the number who had chosen to cut him.

"What is your connection with Dr. Doyle?" Freud asked, as if trying to dispel the impression of curtness in his reply.

"Not a medical one, I assure you. Dr. Doyle has influence with certain literary magazines in England. He writes books more than he practises medicine nowadays, and it is to him that I am indebted for placing my own humble accounts of Holmes's doings with the publishers."

"Ah."

We left the streetcar at the intersection of Wäh-ringer and Bergasse streets and headed east on foot to Dr. Freud's home.

No sooner had we stepped across the threshold than we were made aware of a terrible commotion upstairs. Dimly perceived as we raced past them were the maid, Paula, and a woman who was subsequently introduced to me as Frau Freud. At the time I barely noticed a girl of about five who was clutching the bannister posts in anxiety. Later I was to become friends with little Anna Freud, but at the moment there was no time for introductions. Freud and I dashed into the room where Holmes was frantically pulling apart the carpet-bag, his collar half off and his hair disarranged by the energy of his efforts, coupled with the spasmodic jerkings of one whose muscles are no longer under complete control.

Upon our entering the room, he spun round to face us with wild eyes.

"Where is it?" he shrieked. "What have you done with it?"

It required the efforts of both of us to subdue him, and what followed was a descent into a hell deeper and more awesome than the cauldron of Reichenbach I have tried to describe.

Sometimes the hypnosis would work and sometimes it would not. Sometimes it could be achieved by giving Holmes a sedative beforehand, but this Freud was unwilling to do if there was a chance of achieving success without it.

"He must not begin relying on the sedative," he explained over a hasty meal, shared together in his study.

Of course it was necessary that one of us stand guard constantly to see that Holmes did no injury to himself or to others during the time when he could not be held accountable for his actions. He grew to hate the sight of each of us, and of Paula as well, who, though he terrified her, nevertheless went about her business with determination and every outward appearance of goodwill and unconcern. Dr. Freud and his household could understand Holmes's revilings and not take them to heart, painful and insulting though they might be, but his interminable abuse struck much more deeply into me. I had not thought him capable of such rhetoric or such vituperation. When I appeared in the room to keep him company and watch over him, he heaped on me such execrations as it pains me, even to this day, to recall. He told me how stupid I was, cursed himself for ever having tolerated the companionship of a brainless cripple, and worse. How I bore these taunts, jeers, and insults may best be imagined, but I was not sorry when, on the third day, he tried to rush past me into the corridor and I was obliged to knock him down with a blow made more powerful—I confess it—by the resentment that boiled up within me. I struck him so hard he lapsed into unconsciousness, which horrified me, and as I called for help, I literally beat my breast for the lack of control I had exhibited.

"Do not dwell on it, Doctor." Freud patted me on the arm after we had taken him to his bed. "Every hour that he remains unconscious increases our chances. You saved me from a session of hypnotism and, from what you describe, I am not certain it will work any longer."

That night Holmes awoke in a high fever and was delirious. As Freud and I sat by his bedside, each restraining the movements of his hands, he babbled of oysters overrunning the world and similar nonsense.* Freud listened with the greatest attention.

"Is he fond of oysters?" he demanded of me during a quiet interval. I shrugged, too confused to answer accurately.

During the night our watch was relieved by Paula, and once by Frau Freud. She was a most appealing woman, possessed, like her husband, of a pair of black, sad eyes, but also of a humourous delicate mouth whose firmness suggested inner resources and quiet strength of character.

At one point I apologized to her for the inconvenience and disruption Holmes and I had caused her household.

"I too have read your accounts of Herr Holmes's cases," she replied simply. "It is well-known that your friend is a worthy and courageous man. He needs help now, as *our* friend did." I assumed she referred to the unfortunate friend mentioned in Freud's piece in *Lancet*. "This time we will not fail," she asserted.

Holmes's fever and delirium persisted for three more days, during which it was virtually impossible to get any nourishment inside him. It was exhausting to us—even when we had rested—to be around him, for his convulsive energy was enervating simply to watch. For six hours on the evening of the third day his twitchings and ravings were so alarming that

---

* Oysters held some importance in Holmes's unconscious. When shamming delirium in "The Adventure of the Dying Detective," he worries that the world will be overrun by oysters. Possibly he was incorporating features of his genuine delirium as reported to him afterwards by Watson into his performance. Holmes was also known to eat oysters and appears to have enjoyed them very much. Did consuming them represent an attempt on his part to dominate them and so master his fear? In any case, it would be interesting to learn the origin of the phobia.

I became convinced an onset of brain fever was imminent. When I expressed this view to Sigmund Freud, however, he shook his head.

"The symptoms are very similar," he agreed, "but I think there is no brain fever to be feared here. We are witnessing the final throes of the drug's hold on him. His habit is being torn from his body. If he survives this, he will have reached the turning point on the road to recovery."

"Survives?"

"Men have been known to die of it," he responded shortly.

I sat beside the bed and watched helplessly as the terrible spasms and shrieks continued unabated except for brief intervals that seemed to serve no other purpose than to renew his nervous energies. Towards midnight Dr. Freud insisted that I try to get some rest, pointing out that I could not possibly be of use to my friend in this, his greatest hour of trial. Unwillingly I returned to my own room.

Sleep was impossible. Even had I not been able to hear the detective's piercing screams and wails through the walls, the simple knowledge of the torture he was enduring was enough to keep me awake. Was it worth it? Was there no other way of saving him except by so severe a trial that he might die in attempting to live? I am not a praying man, and I sensed the hypocrisy of my gesture; nevertheless, I knelt and grovelled before the Creator of all things—whoever and whatever he might be—and begged him in the humblest terms that came to mind to spare my friend. I cannot say with certainty what effect my prayers had on Holmes; but they proved sufficiently distracting to ease me into a fitful sleep.

On the fourth day following the onset of his fever

and delirium, Sherlock Holmes woke, seemingly calm and with a normal temperature.

As I entered the room, assuming Paula's place, he eyed me with a mellow languor.

"Watson?" he asked, in a voice so feeble that I should never have taken it for his. "Is that you?"

I assured him that it was, drew up a chair next to the bed, examined him, and informed him that his fever had broken.

"Oh?" His reply was listless.

"Yes. You are on your way to recovery, my dear fellow."

"Oh."

He continued to stare at me, or past me rather, with a vacant expression and no seeming knowledge of where he was and no curiosity about how he came to be there.

He did not object when I took his pulse, which was fearfully weak, but steady; nor did he resist the tray that Frau Freud herself brought up to him. He ate sparingly and only with much nagging encouragement. He apparently wished to eat, yet he had to be reminded the food was before him. This lethargic turn of events, following as it did his violent outbursts and fevered delirium, I found more sinister than anything that had preceded it.

It was not to Freud's liking, either, when he returned from his rounds and inspected his resident patient. He frowned and walked to the window through which could be seen the spires of St. Stephen's—a view, by the way, he cordially loathed. I patted Holmes's hand reassuringly and joined the doctor at the window.

"Well?"

"He appears to have thrown off the addiction," Freud said quietly, in a neutral voice. "He may of course resume it at any time. Such is the curse of enslavement to drugs. It would be interesting to know," he added, with seeming irrelevancy, "how he became involved with cocaine."

"I have always known him to keep it about his rooms," I answered truthfully. "He says he takes it because of boredom, lack of activity."

Freud turned and smiled at me, his features displaying the infinite and nameless wisdom and compassion I had noticed the moment I first set eyes on him.

"That is not the reason a man pursues such a path to destruction," said he softly. "However—"

"What is it that worries you?" I demanded, trying to keep my own voice down. "You say we have weaned him from the fiend."

"Temporarily," Freud repeated, returning to the window, "but we appear also to have weaned him from his spirit. There is an old proverb that suggests that the cure is sometimes more deadly than the disease."

"But what could we do?" I expostulated. "Allow him to poison himself?"

Freud turned round again with a finger on his lips.

"I know." He patted my shoulder and walked back to where the patient lay.

"How do you feel?" he enquired gently, smiling down at my friend. Holmes glanced up at him, and then his eyes glazed over, staring into nothingness.

"Not well."

"Do you remember Professor Moriarty?"

"My evil genius?" The faintest trace of a smile tugged at the corners of his mouth.

"What about him?"

"I know what you want me to say, Doctor. Very well, I shall oblige you: the only time Professor Moriarty truly occupied the role of my evil genius was when it took him three weeks to make clear to me the mysteries of elementary calculus."

"I am not so much interested in your saying it," the doctor responded quietly, "but in your understanding it to be true."

There was a pause.

"I understand it," Holmes whispered at length. In that almost inaudible reply was all the exhausted humiliation and suffering it is possible for a human being to know. Even Freud, who could be as dogged as Holmes, when he felt the occasion demanded it, was loath to break the long silence which followed this terrible confession.

It was Holmes himself who finally brought his reverie to an end; gazing about the room, he espied me, and his features came to life.

"Watson? Come closer, old friend. You are my old friend, are you not?" he added, uncertainly.

"You know I am."

"Ah, yes." He eased back onto the pillows from the sitting posture he had made such an effort to assume, and regarded me with a troubled expression clouding his usually keen grey eyes. "I do not remember much of the past few days," he began, but I cut him off with a gesture of my hand.

"It is over and done with. Do not think about what has happened. It is over."

"I say I do not remember much," he persisted tenaciously, "but I do seem to recall screaming at you, hurling all sorts of epithets in your direction." He smiled in what was meant to be ingratiating self-deprecation. "Did I do that, Watson? Or did I just imagine it?"

"You just imagined it, my dear fellow. Lie back now."

"Because if I did do that," he pursued, obeying my instructions, "I want you to know that I did not mean it. Do you hear me? I did not mean it. I remember distinctly calling you Iscariot. Will you forgive me for that monstrous calumny? Will you?"

"Holmes, I beg of you!"

"You'd better leave him now," Freud interposed, laying a hand on my shoulder. "He is going to sleep."

I rose and fled from the room, my eyes blind with tears.

9

Concerning a Game of Tennis and a Violin

As Sigmund Freud had warned me, though Holmes no longer appeared to crave cocaine, vigilance regarding the drug and possible access to it must remain as strict as before. I had briefly entertained the notion of returning to England, conceiving that the worst was over—which Dr. Freud assured me it was—but he pleaded with me to remain. Holmes's spirits were still alarmingly low, it was still difficult to get him to eat, and it was still impossible yet to send him back to his own world; he so plainly needed a friend that I consented to stay a while.

Another exchange of telegrams took place between my wife and me, during which I outlined the situation and begged her indulgence and she, for her part, responded all warmth and encouragement, saying that the practise was being ably cared for by Cullingworth and that she would inform Mycroft Holmes of his brother's progress.

Holmes's progress, however, was minimal. If he took no further interest in the drug, neither did he evince curiosity regarding anything else. We forced him to eat and cajoled him into taking strolls in the parks near the Hofburg. On these occasions he promenaded dutifully, though he kept his eyes on the ground before him and looked almost nowhere else. I did not know whether to be pleased or not by this development; certainly it was in character with the Holmes I knew so well, who rarely noticed scenery and much preferred to study footprints. Yet when I endeavoured to draw him out on the subject, and asked him what he was able to deduce from the ground, he responded with a tired injunction not to patronize him, and said no more.

He now took his meals with the rest of the household, sitting silent through all attempts we made at conversation, and eating little. Dr. Freud's discussion of other patients appeared to hold no interest for him whatever, and I am afraid I was so preoccupied with Holmes's slightest reactions that I scarcely heard anything of the doctor's cases, either. I have a dim recollection that he referred to them by the strangest names, sometimes alluding to the "Rat Man" or the "Wolf Man," and sometimes to a person called "Anna O." I understood him to be protecting the true identities of these people for reasons of professional discretion, yet I do think he betrayed an otherwise latent sense of humour in the sobriquets he applied to describe them, or at least a real talent for anthropomorphic association. Often, falling asleep with my thoughts idly touching on this and that, I have recalled those snatches of table talk in the Freud home and smiled to think of the man who looked like a rat and the one who resembled a wolf. And what of Anna O? Was she perhaps sensationally rotund?

Curiously, the only member of the household who appeared to elicit any positive response in Holmes was another Anna, Freud's small daughter. She was an adorable child (I am not normally fond of

children),* intelligent and also engaging. After the
first day, Holmes's fits lost whatever terror they had
once held for her and she approached him quite
freely. With some instinct of her own, she was
always quiet in her advances, but they were advances nonetheless. Once, after supper, she offered
to show him her doll collection. With a grave
demeanour, punctiliously polite, Holmes accepted
her invitation and they withdrew to the cupboard
where the figures were assembled. I was on the
point of rising from my chair and following them
when Freud signalled to me to remain where I was.

"We must not suffocate him with our attentions,"
he smiled.

"Nor Anna," laughed Frau Freud, and rang for
more coffee.

The next morning, as I lay in my bed rubbing
the sleep from my eyes, I was startled to hear the
sound of voices from the next room. I looked at my
watch on the night-table and ascertained that it was
not quite eight. From the sounds downstairs I knew
Paula to be in the kitchen and the rest of the family
not yet awake. Who could it be?

Silently I stole towards the door of our adjoining
rooms and peeped through the crack. Holmes was
sitting up in bed talking quietly with little Anna,
who had seated herself at the foot of it. I could not
make it out but the conversation appeared to be a
pleasant one, the child posing questions and Holmes
doing his best to answer them. Once I heard him
chuckle and I crept back from the door lest some
inadvertent sound on my part disturb their rapport.

Following breakfast, Holmes elected to remain in
the study with the object of reading some of the

---

* Does his declaration suggest a reason why Watson
never mentions his children, not even to state that he
fathered any?

Dostoievski (should he come upon any in French translation), rather than accompany us to the Maumberg, Freud's exclusive club, for some indoor tennis.

"Dr. Watson will confirm my utter disregard of exercise for its own sake," he said, smiling, as we hesitated at the door, urging him once more to join us. "You really must not ascribe my staying behind to any motives connected with my illness."

Freud decided not to insist, and leaving Holmes in the care of the ladies—Frau Freud, Paula, and little Anna—we set forth.

The Maumberg, located south of the Hofburg, was a rather different club from those I knew in London. It was primarily a place for exercise, the cafes of the city supplying the social and intellectual deficiencies of the institution.

There was a restaurant and bar, to be sure, but Freud was not in the habit of lingering at either or socializing with the members. He enjoyed a game of tennis, he told me, and simply used the club's courts for their elementary recreational purpose. I was not a tennis player, myself (my arm* having made the question of playing an impossibility), but I wished to see the club and to escape, for a little while, the dreary influence of Holmes's battle which had kept me in constant attendance and depression. Dr. Freud had no doubt sensed this in extending his kind invitation.

The tennis courts were enclosed in a huge wrought-iron structure rather like a green-house. Enormous skylights permitted the sun to brighten the place, while from within it was heated for comfort during the cold months. The courts themselves were constructed of highly polished wood that

---

* Arm? This manuscript does not resolve our doubts concerning the famous Afghan wound.

reverberated in a roaring cacophony as the balls from several simultaneous games struck the flooring.

As we entered the dressing-room where the doctor kept his tennis costume, we passed a group of young fellows who were drinking beer from tall tapered glasses, their feet propped on benches and towels draped carelessly about their necks. We walked by. I heard one of their number choke on his drink and laugh.

"*Juden* in the Maumberg! I say, this place has gone to the dogs since last I set foot here."

Freud, walking ahead of me, stopped and faced the young man, who pretended to be absorbed in conversation with another companion, though indeed they could neither of them suppress their giggling. When he turned to us with a blandly inquisitive expression, I could not but start at his features. His otherwise handsomely cold countenance was made positively sinister by a hideous, livid sabre cut on his left cheek. Indeed, his entire face was transformed by this dreadful wound into something quite malignant, and his icy, unblinking eyes gave him the unpleasant air of a great nodding bird of prey. He was not yet thirty, but the wickedness in that face was ageless.

"Were you referring to me?" Freud demanded quietly, stepping up to where he sat lounging.

"I beg your pardon?" He was all innocence, and his cruel mouth was wreathed in smiles, but his eyes remained expressionless.

"It might interest you to know, *mein Herr,* that since you have last set foot here—which apparently was never, since you appear totally ignorant of the composition of this club, to say nothing of its manners—the membership has become more than a third Jewish." He spun on his heel to go, leaving a trail of good-humoured laughter in his wake. The young man with the scar flushed crimson and listened with bent head to the whisperings of his companion as his eyes followed the departing figure of Freud.

"Dr. Freud, is it?" he called after him suddenly. "Not the same Dr. Freud who was asked to leave the staff of the Allgemeines Krankenhaus because of his charming assertion that young men sleep with their mothers? By the way, Doctor, did you sleep with your mother?"

The doctor froze during this speech, then turned around again, very pale, and faced his tormentor.

"You are absurd," he replied briefly, and turned once more to go, again having hit the mark he desired. In an instant the beer drinker was on his feet, dashing his glass to bits on the floor in a fury.

"Will you step out, *mein Herr*?" he cried in a voice shaking with rage. "My seconds will call upon you at your convenience."

Freud looked him up and down, a smile twitching at the corners of his mouth.

"Come, come," he offered blandly, "you know that gentlemen do not duel with Jews. Have you no sense of etiquette?"

"You refuse? Do you know who I am?"

"I neither know nor care. I'll tell you what I will do," Freud went on, before the other could protest, "I'll undertake to beat you in a set of tennis. Will that satisfy your sense of propriety?"

At this juncture some of the young man's friends sought to intervene, but he pushed them vehemently away, never taking his eyes from Freud, who was now coolly engaged in removing his boots and taking down his tennis racquet.

"Very well, *Doktor*. I shall attend you on the courts."

"I shall not keep you waiting," responded Freud, without bothering to look up.

Advance word of the match had obviously run through the club by the time we made our appearance beneath the enormous skylights and joined the young man with the scar and his entourage, some of whom were elaborately examining the balls to be used as if they were bullets.

"Don't you find this absurd?" I tried to caution Freud as we started up the stairs.

"I find it entirely absurd," he replied without hesitation, "but not so absurd as our attempting to slay one another."

"You do not fear losing this match?"

"My dear Doctor, it is only a game."

It may have been a game to Freud, but his opponent was in deadly earnest and showed it from the moment play began. He was bigger, stronger, and in far better training than the physician and they were both aware of the fact. He drove his shots deep and with considerable accuracy, while Freud answered them as best he could but appeared in no way discomfited when he was not in time to return them. In this fashion he gave up the first two games, capturing only one or two points in the process.

During the third game he did slightly better and actually reached deuce before surrendering the point. I took it upon myself to draw some water for the doctor as the play was halted for the switching of sides.

"You did rather better that last round," I noted encouragingly as I handed him the sponge.

"I hope to do better still." Freud made a few passes with the sponge behind his neck. "His game is only offensive and, among other things, without a backhand. Have you noticed?"

I shook my head.

"But it is the truth. Every point I've drawn from him has been to his backhand. Watch."

I watched, as did two hundred* eager spectators. Now the tide turned, slowly but inexorably, as Freud took game after game away from the younger man. At first his opponent could not understand what was happening. It was not until the score was tied at three games all that he realized Freud's strategy was deliberate, and, knowing his own weakness, stood farther and farther to the left of the court, in hopes of forestalling the doctor's tactics. In this manner he gained a point or two, but Freud quickly perceived his intentions and frustrated them by shooting his returns down the right-hand alley, far from the reach of his harried opponent.

And when he did reach them in time, Freud exploited the exposed backhand once more, hitting deftly cross court again. The playing was not easy, but the young man with the scar clearly had the worst of it. Forcing a defensive game, Freud obliged him to race from side to side, whilst he himself stood virtually still. Anger led the young ruffian into errors he should never have made had he been in full control of his temper, and Freud drew the set to a close within an hour, the final score standing at six games to three.

When the last shot had spun wide of the young man's reach, Freud walked calmly up to the net.

"Is honour satisfied?" he enquired politely. I be-

---

* Watson's memory surely plays him false here. A personal inspection of the Maumberg's yet extant indoor courts reveals that no more than one hundred spectators could have watched this exciting though little-known episode in Freud's life. Obviously Freud's biographer, Ernest Jones, was not among them.

lieve the other would have sprung forward and throttled him there and then, had not his friends hastily intercepted and held him back by force.

In the dressing chambers, Freud bathed and changed once more into his street clothes without comment, except to acknowledge my effusive congratulations, and we started back to Bergasse 19.

"At least I had my set of tennis," he observed, hailing a cab. "And I didn't even have to wait for a court."

"That man's comment—about your theory," I asked, after some hesitation. "You don't seriously contend that boys—that they—"

He smiled at me with that expression of sadness I had come to know so well.

"Set your mind at rest, Doctor. I do not contend that at all."

I sank back on the cushions of the cab with something like a sigh, though I do not think Freud was aware of it.

When we returned to the house, Freud cautioned me to say nothing of the tennis-duel to Holmes. He did not wish to distract my friend with the incident, and I agreed.

We found the detective where we had left him, poring over volumes in the study and not inclined to talk. Merely finding that he took an interest in something was encouraging to me. Withdrawing to my room, I pondered over the curious scene at the Maumberg. We never had learned that young jabbernowl's name, but his face, his livid wicked face, seamed with that evil scar, lingered in my mind for the rest of the afternoon.

During supper Sherlock Holmes appeared to have relapsed into his former malaise. Despite our efforts at conversation, his rejoinders were again monosyllabic and desultory in the extreme. I eyed Freud anxiously but he affected to ignore my glances and chattered away as though nothing were amiss.

Following supper he rose and excused himself from the table, returning some moments later with a parcel in his arms.

"Herr Holmes, I have something which I believe you might enjoy," said he, handing over the oblong box.

"Oh?"

Holmes took the box and left it in his lap, not knowing, apparently, what to do with it.

"I wired to England for this," Freud went on, seating himself again. Holmes still said nothing, but looked at the box.

"May I help you open it?" offered Anna, reaching up for the string.

"Please do," Holmes responded, and turned the box round towards the child.

"Be careful," her father enjoined as her small fingers grappled with the knot. "Here." With a pocket-knife, Freud severed the string and Anna pulled open the paper, then uncovered the box. Involuntarily I drew in my breath when I saw what was inside.

"It's another box!" Anna exclaimed.

"Let Herr Holmes open this one himself," Frau Freud commanded behind me.

"Well, aren't you going to?" Anna encouraged him.

Without answering her, Holmes drew a case from the stuffing inside the box. Slowly but automatically, his fingers worked the catches and he withdrew the Stradivarius, then looked up at the Viennese physician.

"This is very kind of you," he said in the same quiet tone that so frightened me. Anna clapped her hands with excitement.

"It's a fiddle!" she cried, "a fiddle! Can you play it? Oh, please, won't you play it for me? Please?"

Holmes looked down at her, then back at the instrument in his hands. Its varnish gleamed in the gas-light. He plucked a string or two, wincing slightly at the sound. Tucking the violin beneath his chin, he jerked his neck up and down to accustom the thing to its proper place and set about tuning it. This done—as we watched with all the breathless anticipation of people at the circus witnessing a high-wire performance—he withdrew the bow and ran some rosin up and down it after tightening the horsehair.

"Hmm."

He played tentatively at first, and not at all in his usual style as he assayed a few chords and phrases. Slowly, however, a smile spread across his features—the first genuinely happy expression I had beheld there in what seemed an eternity.

And then he began to play in earnest.

I have alluded elsewhere to my friend's musical accomplishments, but never did he so excel himself and bewitch his listeners as he did that night. A miracle took place before our very eyes as the instrument restored life to its owner and he to it.

Seemingly without realizing it, Holmes pushed back his chair and arose, still playing the violin and becoming more animated as he became increasingly absorbed. I forget what he began with—I am not musically knowledgeable myself, as some of my readers have observed before this—but I fancy it was some exercises and wistful compositions of his own.

I know what he played, next, however. Holmes had a flair for the dramatic and he knew, after all, where he was.

He played Strauss waltzes. Oh, how he played!

Rich, languorous, sonorous, gay, propulsively rhythmic—I know they were propulsively rhythmic because Dr. Freud seized his wife round the waist and began to waltz her about the dining-room and into the sitting-room as Holmes, Anna, Paula, and myself followed. So enrapt was I in watching the spectacle and eyeing my friend, whose smile had not ceased to leave his face, that it was some moments before I became aware of a small hand tugging at my sleeve. I looked down and beheld Anna, who stretched forth her arms in my direction.

I was never accounted much of a dancer, and with my game leg I was perhaps still less of one than most unmusical men—but I danced. It wasn't, I suspect, a very graceful performance, but it possessed infinite energy and good-will.

"Tales of the Vienna Woods," "Wiener Blut," the "Blue Danube," "Wine, Women, and Song"— Holmes played them all as we four whirled around the room, shrieking with laughter and enjoyment! After a time I exchanged partners with Freud and danced with his wife, while the doctor—whom I could perceive was little more accustomed to waltzing than I—gambolled about with his daughter. At one point, in my excitement, I even recall spinning Paula about, much to her amusement and over her protestations.

When at last it was over, we all of us fell into chairs, gasping for breath, our ridiculous smiles playing on, though the music that inspired them had stopped. Holmes removed the violin from beneath his chin and stared at it for a long time. Then he looked up and across the room at Freud.

"I have not ceased to be astounded by your talents," Freud said to him.

"I am just beginning to be amazed by yours," Holmes countered, looking him steadily in the eye

—and there, I delighted to observe, was the familiar sparkle.

I retired that night marvelling at the power of music. I believe it is somewhere in *Julius Caesar* * that the bard speaks of music having the power to soothe the savage breast and calm the restless spirit, but I had never had the opportunity of witnessing a practical demonstration of that phenomenon.

It persisted after the rest of the house had gone to bed, as I had good reason to know, for through the thin partition that divided Holmes's room from mine I could hear him quietly scraping away on into the wee hours. Allowed to choose his own repertoire, he reverted to the melancholy, dreamy airs of his own invention. They were haunting and desperately sad, but they had the eventual effect of lulling me gently to sleep. I drifted off vaguely wondering if, now that we had managed to strike a spark in my friend's chilly soul, that spark was destined to kindle itself into flame, or rather to die out again with the coming day. The episode with the violin proved that his soul was not gutted and charred beyond igniting, but whether music was sufficient in itself for the purpose, this I instinctively doubted. Somewhere, too, in my uneasy slumbers, I saw again that devil's scheming face with its grotesque, dead white wound.

---

* It isn't.

10

A Study in Hysteria

Sherlock Holmes was quiet the next morning at breakfast. He gave no clue as to whether or not the musical episode had well and truly set him on the road to recovery. Dr. Freud remained inscrutable in the face of his patient's neutral behaviour. He asked, as usual, how Holmes had slept and if he would like a second cup of coffee.

What happened next forever prevents my saying with certainty whether or not the violin alone recalled my companion to his former self. If the doorbell had not rung, the mad adventure into which we fell headlong would not have occurred. Yet, in spite of what followed, I am glad the messenger arrived with a note for Dr. Freud, for without it I fear Holmes might well have relapsed, fiddle or no.

He was a courier from the Allgemeines Krankenhaus, the teaching hospital to which Freud had once been attached. He bore a note from somebody on the staff, asking if Dr. Freud would care to come and look at a patient who had arrived the night before. The note had a familiar flavour as Freud read it aloud.

"I would be pleased if you could spare the time to consult with me about a most peculiar case (it ran). The patient cannot or will not speak a word, and though she is frail, her health appears perfectly sound. Could you find a moment to stop by and conduct a brief examination? Your methods are a little off the beaten track but I have always respected them, myself." It was signed "Schultz."

"You see what a pariah I am," Freud said, smiling, as he folded the note. "Would you care to accompany me, gentlemen, and see the recalcitrant woman?"

"I should be greatly interested," Holmes responded with alacrity, and proceeded to fold his napkin. Preparing to go as well, I remarked humourously that I had not thought the doctor's patients could be of any interest to him. He certainly had not evinced curiosity about them before.

"Oh, I have no interest in the patient," Holmes laughed, "but doesn't this Dr. Schultz sound much like our old friend Lestrade? * I have decided to come and offer Doctor Freud my sympathy."

It was no great distance to the hospital, and on arriving we were informed that Dr. Schultz was with his patient in the Psychiatric Wing. We found him in the outside court, accessible through a separate gate, beyond which the patients were permitted—under supervision—to sit or wander about in the sun. There were games also at their disposal and some half dozen were playing croquet, though it was a mad game they played, with much shouting and noise and need for the attendants' presence.

---

* Holmes refers here to Inspector G. Lestrade of Scotland Yard, who—like a number of other detectives at the Yard—was fond of denigrating Holmes's methods and theories, until it was necessary to call him for help when a case proved too complex for an ordinary mind to handle.

Dr. Schultz was a heavy-set and seemingly self-important individual, roughly fifty years of age, with a thin mustache and incongruously large side-whiskers.

He greeted Freud with guarded formality and Holmes and myself in a perfunctory manner. As the hospital was devoted to teaching as well as the practice of medicine, he did not demur when Freud asked if we might accompany him. I believe he caught the fact that I was a physician and assumed that we had reasons of our own for wishing to view the patient.

"It's really no concern of mine," Schultz explained as we stepped briskly over the lawn, "but we must do something with her, you see. She was observed attempting to throw herself into the canal from the Augarten Bridge. Bystanders tried to stop her, but she succeeded in breaking free and throwing herself in anyway. Malnutrition," he added, as an after-thought, "but when the police brought her round she did eat a little. The question is: what now? If you can find out who she is or anything of the kind, I shall be forever in your debt."

He did not sound much interested in being forever in Freud's debt, and Freud smiled at me rather than responding directly.

I was struck—as Holmes had been by Schultz's message—with the similarity in tone between the proper physician and the proper Scotland Yard investigator when dealing with their respective iconoclasts. Whatever Freud's theories, they resembled Holmes's in the condescending scepticism they evoked in quarters of officialdom and sanctioned thought.

"There she is—all yours. I am due in surgery. Just leave word for me at my office, if you will be so kind. I will look in on her again tomorrow."

He departed for his operation, leaving us to face a young woman who sat in a basket-chair, looking out at the lawn with wide unblinking blue eyes that refused to squint in the bright sunlight. She was obviously under-nourished and her skin had a delicate blue tint, especially beneath the eyes. It might have been a striking face but for the ravages of her condition. I should have said she was exhausted, had not the rigid quality of her posture proclaimed that she was under the highest tension.

Freud walked round her slowly as Holmes and I watched. He passed a hand before her face. There was no response. She did not resist as he gently held her wrist to gauge her pulse, but when he released his hold, the limb dropped back into her lap like a dead thing. Her face was thin, thinner even than it was supposed to be judging from its bone structure. We were unable to estimate her weight since she was dressed in ample hospital clothing. Holmes appeared mildly interested in the woman and stood watching attentively as Freud went about his cursory examination.

"You see why they call for me," Freud said quietly. "They don't know what else to do. She cannot be sent to any of the normal facilities for the destitute in her present condition."

"What made her hysterical?" I asked.

"That is not beyond surmise, surely. Poverty, despair, desertion. At the end of her tether, she decided to end her life, and, being deprived of that goal, she retreats into the state in which we find her."

Freud was opening his black bag and rummaging about for something. He took out a syringe and a bottle.

"What will you do?" Holmes squatted down beside him on his haunches, not removing his eyes from the unfortunate wretch who sat before him.

"What I can," Freud responded, rolling back the floppy sleeve of her white gown and sterilizing a portion of her arm with cotton dipped in alcohol. "I will see if I can hypnotize her. In order to do that I must give her something to relax and enable me to get her attention."

Holmes nodded and rose to his feet as Freud plunged the needle home.

He began swinging his watch-chain back and forth and talking in that solicitous yet forceful voice of his—as I had had occasion to witness so many times before. I cast a brief glance at Holmes, wondering what associations this procedure held for him, but his faculties were plainly absorbed by the woman's reactions to the watch-chain and Freud's voice.

The doctor motioned us with his free hand to stand back, out of the line of the patient's vision, and went on quietly telling her to listen to what he had to say, to relax, that she was among friends, and so forth.

At first I was conscious of the croquet game, with its ludicrous shouts, going on somewhere to my left, but as Freud went on, the sounds receded into the distance. So persuasive was the doctor's insistent litany that we might have been shrouded in the familiar semi-darkness of his study at Bergasse 19.

Almost imperceptibly, the patient's eyes began to blink and then to follow the movements of the fob, which they had hitherto ignored. Perceiving this, Freud changed his quiet injunctions to relax and commanded her, in the same soft tones, to sleep.

Hesitating at first, with another flicker of her lids, the girl did as she was bid, and closed her eyes.

"You can still hear me, can't you?" Freud asked. "Nod your head if you can hear me."

She nodded languidly, her shoulders slumping.

"Now you will be able to talk," Freud told her, "and to answer some very simple questions. Are you ready? Nod again, please."

She did.

"What is your name?"

There was a long pause. Her mouth moved slightly but no sound emerged.

"Please speak more clearly. I will ask you again and you will speak clearly. What is your name?"

"My name is Nancy."

She spoke in English!

Freud frowned in surprise and exchanged a brief involuntary glance with me, then returned his attention to the girl. Coughing slightly, he addressed her now in English.

"Now then, Nancy. What is your full name?"

"I have two names."

"Yes, and what are they?"

"Slater. Nancy Slater. Nancy Osborn Slater. Von Leinsdorf," she added with a choking sound. Her mouth continued to work after she had done speaking.

"All right, Nancy. Relax. Relax. You are all right. Tell me: where are you from?"

"Providence."

Freud looked up at us, clearly mystified, and I confess I was almost of the opinion we were the victims of some improbable practical joke—or was her fancy now wandering idly into the realm of metaphysics?

Holmes solved the dilemma. Standing directly behind the girl he spoke quietly so that only we might hear.

"Perhaps she refers to Providence, the capital of

Rhode Island. It is, I believe, the smallest of the United States."

Freud was nodding energetically before he had concluded, and then, shrugging at the peculiarity of it, he knelt before the girl once more and repeated the question.

"Yes. Providence. Rhode Island."

"What are you doing here?"

"I spent my honeymoon in an attic."

Her mouth was chewing convulsively on itself again, and when she spoke some speech impediment distorted her replies, making it somewhat difficult to catch the words. Perplexed as I was by her condition and her inarticulate speech, my heart nonetheless went out to her, poor stricken creature!

"All right, now. Relax. Relax."

Freud rose and faced us.

"It doesn't make any sense at all."

"Ask some more questions," Holmes prompted quietly. His eyes were hooded like the head of the cobra beneath heavy lids, but I knew he was as far from sleep as he ever got. Only the utmost fascination could provoke that dreamy appearance where the smoke rising from his pipe and the fact that he was standing were the only clues to his consciousness. "Ask her some more questions," he repeated. "Where was she married?"

Freud repeated the question.

"In the meat-house." Her speech impediment made it difficult to understand her.

"A meat-house?"

She nodded. Freud looked over her shoulder at us and shrugged once more. Holmes motioned him to go on.

"You say your name is Von Leinsdorf. Who is Von Leinsdorf? Your husband?"

"Yes."

"Baron Karl Von Leinsdorf?" Freud was unable to suppress the challenging note in his voice.

"Yes."

"The Baron is dead," he began, when the woman who called herself Nancy suddenly rose with a fierce movement, her eyes still closed, but apparently struggling to open.

"NO!"

"Sit down, Nancy. Sit down. That's good. That's very good. Now relax again. Relax."

Once more he rose and faced us.

"This is most peculiar. Obviously her delusions persist under hypnosis—not often the case," he informed us with a significant look.

"Delusions?" Holmes spoke, opening his eyes. "What leads you to infer they are delusions?"

"They make no sense."

"That is not the same thing. Who is Baron Von Leinsdorf?"

"An elderly peer of the realm. A cousin to the Emperor, I believe. He died some weeks ago."

"Was he married?"

"I have no idea. I confess I am at a loss. I have managed to communicate with her but what she has to say does not tell us what should be done with her."

He cupped a fist in a palm and twisted it in his perplexity as we stared down at the strange patient, whose mouth was beginning to work again.

"May I pose a question or two?" Holmes nodded in her direction.

"You?" Freud sounded more surprised by the request than he probably had intended.

"If you don't mind. I may be able to shed some small light in the darkness that surrounds us."

Freud considered the question again, looking keenly at Holmes, who waited for his response with every outward appearance of indifference. Yet I knew from a dozen tell-tale signs, that meant something to me alone, how dearly he wanted to receive the doctor's permission.

"It cannot do any harm," I ventured, "and surely, as you confess yourself mystified, a little assistance might not be amiss. I have known my friend to make sense out of what was far less sensible," I added.

Freud hesitated a moment longer. He was unwilling, I think, to admit defeat or acknowledge his need for help, but he needed help, and I also think he had some inkling of how much it meant to Holmes, who had shown so few signs of life himself, until recently.

"Very well. But be quick. The sedative is wearing off and we shall lose her shortly."

Holmes's eyes gleamed briefly with excitement, but hooded themselves almost at once as he followed Freud to the front of the basket-chair.

"There is someone here who would like to talk to you, Nancy. You may speak as freely to him as you did to me. Are you ready?" Freud bent closer. "Are you ready?"

"Y-yes."

Freud nodded to Holmes, who seated himself on the grass at the foot of the chair and looked up at her. His hands rested in his lap but his finger-tips were pressed together in his accustomed fashion when listening to the statement of a client's case.

"Nancy. Tell me who bound your wrists and ankles," he said. His voice did not need to strive for Freud's gentle quality. With a start, I realized how similar it was to the tone he employed when comforting troubled clients in the sitting room at Baker Street.

"I don't know."

For the first time, Dr. Freud and I noticed the bluish marks around the girl's wrists and ankles.

"They used leather, didn't they?"

"Yes."

"And put you in a garret?"

"What?"

"An attic?"

"Yes."

"How long were you kept there?"

"I—I—"

Freud held up a warning hand and Holmes nodded imperceptibly.

"All right, Nancy. Never mind that question. Tell me: how did you escape? How did you leave the attic?"

"I broke the window."

"With your feet?"

"Yes."

I now noticed the cuts on the back of the girl's feet, exposed in the hospital clogs.

"And then you used the glass to sever your bonds?"

"Yes."

"And you climbed down the drain-pipe?"

Very gently he examined her hands. Now that Holmes drew our attention to it, we could see the torn nails and recent evidences of peeled skin on the palms. Her hands were extraordinarily beautiful otherwise, long, graceful, and well-formed.

"And you fell, didn't you?"

"Yes . . ." There was emotion creeping again into her voice and her lips were starting to bleed, so badly was she mutilating them.

"See here, gentlemen," Holmes stood up and softly pulled back a lock of her rich auburn tresses. Her hair had been tied behind in a knot by the hospital attendants but it had fallen loose and covered a purple bruise.

Freud moved forward and motioned Holmes to cease his interrogations, which he did, stepping back and knocking out the ashes from his pipe.

"Sleep now, Nancy. Go to sleep," Freud ordered.

Dutifully, she closed her eyes.

11

We Visit the Opera

"What does it mean?" demanded Freud. We were sitting in a little cafe on Sensen Gasse, just north of the hospital and the pathology institute, and having cups of delicious Viennese coffee while we pondered the problem of the woman who called herself Nancy Slater Von Leinsdorf.

"It means villainy," Holmes responded quietly. "We do not know how much of her story is true, but it is certain the lady was bound hand and foot and starved in a room that fronted another building in a narrow alley, and she escaped in much the fashion she described. It is a pity the hospital staff cleaned her up and burnt her clothes. Her original condition would have been most helpful."

I stole a glance at Freud, hoping he would not interpret Holmes's remark as a callous one. The detective realized with one part of his brain that it was necessary to care for the woman, that she had been soaking wet and in need of help, but the other part of his brain automatically classed people as mere units in a problem, and at such moments his references to them—before those who were un-

146

familiar with his methods—must always seem surprising.

Dr. Freud, however, was intent on his own line of thought.

"To think that I was prepared to certify her as a complete lunatic," he murmured, "that I could not see—"

"You saw," interrupted Holmes, "but you did not observe. The distinction is an important one and sometimes makes a critical difference."

"But who is she? Is she really from Providence, Rhode Island, or is that part of her fancy?"

"It is a cardinal error to theorize in advance of the facts," Holmes admonished. "Inevitably it biases the judgement."

He lit his pipe as Freud stared at his coffee cup. In the past two hours their positions had been quietly reversed. Hitherto the doctor had been mentor and guide, but now Holmes had assumed that role—easily a more familiar one to him than that of helpless patient. Though his expression remained inscrutable, I knew how keenly he rejoiced in the return to his more familiar self; while Freud, to do him justice, was not averse to playing the part of his pupil.

"What is to be done, then?" he demanded. "Shall we inform the police?"

"She was in the hands of the police when she was discovered," Holmes replied a trifle hastily. "If they did nothing for her then, what should they do now? And what would we tell them, eh? We know only a very little and that little may be too small for them to work with. It would in London," he added drily. "Besides, if there really is a nobleman involved, they may be reluctant to delve too deeply into the business."

"What do you suggest, then?"

Holmes leaned back and made a casual show of studying the ceiling.

"Would you consider looking into the matter yourself?"

"I?" Holmes did his best to appear astonished, but the role was a little too close to life, and I fear that for once he overplayed it. "But surely my condition—"

"Your condition has not incapacitated you, obviously," Freud broke in impatiently. "Besides, work is just what you need."

"Very well." Holmes sat forward abruptly, giving up the game. "First we must find out about Baron Von Leinsdorf—who he was, what he died of, when, and so forth. And, of course, whether or not he possessed a wife, and, if so, of what nationality. Since our client is unable to answer certain questions, we must work the case from its other end."

"What makes you say that the woman's garret faced another building over a narrow alley?" I asked.

"Elementary, my dear fellow. Our client's skin was white as a fish's belly, yet we know from her own statement that there was a window in her prison and that it was large enough to accommodate her escape. Inference: although the room possessed a window, there was something that prevented any great degree of sunlight from entering, for surely, if it had, she would not be so pale. And what more likely to achieve this than another building? It is a longer shot, but we might also infer that the building is a newer one than the one that housed our client, because architects do not usually construct windows opening out onto brick walls."

"Wonderful!" exclaimed Freud, who I could see was taking hope from Holmes's words and from his calm, assured demeanour.

"It is merely a question of associating probabilities in the most probable fashion. For example, in *The Tempest*, the shipwrecked duke and his comrades comment on the strange storm that washed them ashore on Prospero's island and yet failed to dampen their clothing. For years scholars have debated amongst themselves concerning this singular tempest. Some have held that it was a metaphysical storm only, and others have postulated equally intricate symbolic hurricanes, all designed to leave the mariners' clothing dry. Yet it helps to know that the reason this storm did not disarrange the duke's clothing is that costumes were the most expensive part of the Elizabethan theatre's resources and the management could not risk mildew every time the play was performed, to say nothing of the actors falling prey to pneumonia. It is easy to imagine—once one is armed with this knowledge—the Burbages, father and son, requesting their playwright to throw in a line alluding to their dry habiliments after their terrible confrontation with the elements. Is there an Austrian equivalent to Burke's Peerage? Perhaps the afternoon would not be wasted if you were to look up some details regarding the late Baron Von Leinsdorf."

"Let me use you as my sounding board, Watson," said Holmes, after Sigmund Freud had left to conduct his research into the late nobleman's affairs. "I must pick my way carefully—not because we are faced with an insoluble mystery, but because I am like a sailor who has spent too much time ashore, and I must regain my sea legs. Perhaps a walk would help, talking of legs."

We paid our due and set forth towards Währinger Strasse, where we turned right. Holmes had filled his pipe again, and he stopped briefly to light it, concentrating in the slight breeze.

"There are two possibilities here, Watson," said

he. "One is that this woman is who she claims to be, and the other that she is deluded—or else intent on deluding us. Don't look so surprised, my dear fellow; that she is shamming for our benefit is an idea we cannot afford to discount at this stage of the game. Now this question, the question of her identity, we shall leave, as I said, until we have further data. But the other elements in the case are entitled to our speculation. Why was this woman kept in a garret, tied hand and foot? Whether she be princess or beggar woman, there are only two possibilities. Either her abductors wished her to do something, or else they wished to prevent her doing something."

"If she was bound hand and foot," I ventured, "the latter possibility strikes me as more likely."

Holmes looked at me and smiled.

"Possibly, Watson. Possibly. But taking the beggar woman as our working hypothesis, a beggar woman who speaks English with an American accent—what could she do, and to whom, that they should fear her? And if they feared her and wished to prevent her from doing anything, why did they allow her to live at all? Why not simply—" His voice trailed off.

"Holmes, supposing these people—whoever they are—*did* wish to do away with her? Isn't it possible that they drove her deliberately to the suicide she attempted at the canal?"

"You mean allowed her to escape? I think not, Watson. Her flight was too daring, too ingenious, and too risky for her captors to have anticipated it. Remember she slipped coming down the drain-pipe and hurt her head."

We walked for a time in silence. I noticed that we were heading past Dr. Freud's house along Bergasse and moving slowly towards the canal.

"Are you going to look at the Augarten Bridge?" I enquired.

"Of what use is the bridge to us?" he answered impatiently. "We know that the constables found her there and failed to prevent her from throwing herself off it. No, I would rather try to find the building where she was kept. It's deuced awkward having a client who can't talk."

"What makes you think you can find the building?" I gasped. "It could be anywhere in Vienna!"

"No, no, my dear doctor, not anywhere at all. Remember, in her weakened condition, the young lady could not have travelled very far. She was found on the bridge, ergo, she got there from the immediate vicinity. Besides, we have already inferred an alley, and is not a waterfront conducive to that notion? A warehouse, perhaps; with a meathouse nearby? In any case, I am not expecting to find the building. I simply would like to familiarize myself with the general scene of the action."

He fell silent, leaving me to my own thoughts, which, I confess, were utterly confused. I did not like to break in on his contemplations, but the more I considered the matter, the more bewildering it became.

"Holmes, why should a woman take all the trouble to escape and then throw herself into the river at the first opportunity?"

"A fair question, Watson. A tantalizing question, and one that is probably crucial to our case, though there are at present an infinite number of motivations, all of which, I suspect, depend on our establishing the identity of our client."

"Perhaps we are making more of all this than there is," I hazarded, for though I did not wish to deprive my companion of the therapy of the chase, nevertheless, it was best not to nourish false hopes.

"Perhaps she is just an unfortunate victim of an individual, a lover become deranged or—"

"It won't do, Watson," he laughed. "In the first place, the woman is a foreigner. Under hypnosis she answers questions in American English. Then again, we have the mention of a Baron Von Leinsdorf— surely not a small fish. And finally," he said, turning to me, "what matter if the case is only a small one? It has its own peculiar rewards, and there is no reason why this unhappy woman should have less justice than the wealthier or more influential specimens of her sex."

This time I said no more, but accompanied him in silence as we entered a section of the city which was considerably less agreeable than those neighbourhoods we had seen during our stay.

The houses were no more than two stories high, built of wood rather than stone. They were dirty, many of them needing paint, and all tended down towards the canal where they stopped just short of the water's edge. There, dilapidated dories were beached on the rocky terrain, looking like stranded small whales. Short telegraph poles with sagging wires completed the dismal picture, and the canal itself added the final touch. Muddy, sluggish, and crammed with unattractive barges—for Vienna received most of its supplies by water—it was a sight more reminiscent of sections of the Thames than of the city of the beautiful blue Danube, which lay some miles to the east, beyond our field of vision.

Here and there a warehouse and a short pier dotted the endless stretch of tenements, and occasional shouts of laughter and the wheezings of an accordion proclaimed a seedy public house in the vicinity—a far cry from the luxury of the Cafe Griensteidl. Off to our right some quarter of a mile lay the Augarten Bridge where the adventure had begun.

"A dreary enough vicinity," Holmes commented, surveying the bleak scene, "and any one of those buildings might accommodate our structural specifications for Nancy Slater's prison."

"Nancy Slater?"

"For want of another name, that one must serve," he returned equably. "I am not a medical man and so cannot properly refer to her as the patient; client, too, seems inappropriate, under the circumstances. She is not in a position, after all, to communicate with us, much less to engage our services in her behalf. Shall we be getting back? I believe Dr. Freud has kindly arranged for us to attend the opera this evening. I am dying to hear Vitelli, though they do say he is past his prime. In any case, I must make sure that the evening clothes you purchased for me will fit."

So saying, we turned in our tracks and trudged out of that weary place. Holmes said little on our way home, though he stopped at a telegraph office and despatched a wire. Knowing him as well as I did, I made no attempt to intrude upon his thoughts, but busied myself with the problem at hand, trying without success not to reason in advance of the facts, but it was a hopeless effort and I gave it up as a bad job. My mind was not logical and disciplined, as was my companion's; it was ever straying to romantic, and utterly improbable solutions to the affair, none of which I should have the courage to broach to any hearer but myself.

I had succeeded completely in one task, however: I knew Sherlock Holmes's measurements and had even allowed for an inch or two less in view of his emaciated condition. The clothes I ordered from Horn's, the smart tailor in the Stephenplaz, fitted the detective beautifully.

Dr. Freud was already at home when we returned, and waited for us with the information Holmes himself would normally have run to earth had he been familiar with the city and its language. His search had taken no little time, yet he had managed to see a patient later in the afternoon. "Wolf Man," "Rat Man," or whatever, he was always conscientious about them.

Baron Karl Helmut Wolfgang Von Leinsdorf (Freud told us) was a second cousin to the Emperor Franz Josef, on his mother's side. He himself was from Bavaria, not Austria, and the bulk of his estate—which consisted of factories devoted to the manufacture of armaments and munitions—was located in the Ruhr Valley of Germany.

The Baron had been a pillar—albeit a reclusive one—of Viennese society. He was devoted to the theatre. He had been married twice, first to a lesser Hapsburg princess, who had died some twenty years before, leaving him with an only son as heir.

Young Manfred Gottfried Karl Wolfgang Von Leinsdorf enjoyed a rather less savoury reputation than his late father. A prodigal, his gaming debts were said to be enormous, and his character—particularly where women were concerned—was known to be totally unscrupulous. He had been to Heidelberg for three years, but left that seat of learning somewhat under a cloud. His political views were extremely conservative and favoured a return to—

"And the second marriage?" Holmes interrupted quietly.

Freud sighed.

"Was made two months before his death. On a voyage to America he made the acquaintance of the Providence textile heiress, Nancy Osborn Slater. They were married almost at once."

"Why the rush?" Holmes wondered aloud. "Surely people of means and station habitually prolong the ritual of betrothal and matrimony for all the festivity it is worth."

"The Baron was nearly seventy," Freud responded, shrugging. "Perhaps—in view of his death, which occurred so soon after the nuptials—he had an inkling—"

"Quite so, quite so. Curiouser and curiouser," my companion added, forgetting his grammar * and sitting back in his evening clothes with his long legs stretched towards the fire in Freud's study, his eyes gleaming beneath half-closed lids. His finger-tips were judiciously pressed together, as his custom was when he wished to concentrate.

"They returned to Europe on the cutter *Alicia* † sometime in mid-March," Freud resumed, "and went straight to the Baron's villa in Bavaria—a virtually inaccessible retreat, I am told—where the Baron died some three weeks ago."

"A little more than two months," Holmes pondered. Then, opening his eyes, he asked: "Were you able to determine the cause of death?"

Freud shook his head.

"He was no longer young, as I have said."

"But in good health?"

"So far as I was able to learn."

"That is interesting."

---

* Holmes, in my opinion, was not forgetting his grammar, as Watson suggests, but rather quoting from *Alice in Wonderland*, by Lewis Carroll. Watson was obviously unfamiliar with the book (he preferred sea stories) or else had forgotten it.

† By an odd coincidence it was the inexplicable disappearance of this same ship some years later that Watson lists among Holmes's unsolved cases.

"But hardly conclusive," I interposed. "After all, when an elderly man—even one enjoying the benefits of good health—takes a wife less than half his age—"

"That is a point which I have considered," Holmes replied coldly, then turned again to Freud. "And what has become of the widow?"

Freud hesitated.

"I have been unable to learn. Though she appears to be living here in Vienna, she is apparently even more of a recluse than her late husband."

"Which means she may not be here at all," I suggested.

There was a silence as Holmes contemplated this information, docketing it in the appropriate pigeon-hole of his brain.

"Perhaps," he conceded, "though such a seclusion is of course understandable. She is in mourning, knows few people in this country—unless she has been here before—and she speaks little or no German. Certainly she has not spent any time in Vienna."

He rose and looked at his watch.

"Doctor, is your wife prepared to join us? I believe you said the curtain was at half-past eight?"

Too much has been written about the fabled Vienna Opera House—and by more eloquent pens than mine—for me to attempt a description of that fabulous theatre. Yet I, visiting it in the heyday of its elegance, and at the zenith of Vienna's opulence, had never beheld such concentrated magnificence as was exhibited that night. The sparkling chandeliers were only to be compared with the jewelry worn by the gorgeously apparelled ladies in the audience. How I wish Mary could have seen the sight! Diamonds shone on brocade, on velvet, and on silken skin, so that the spectators may truly be said to have rivalled the spectacle.

The opera being given that night was something or other of Wagner's, but I cannot remember for the life of me just what it was. Holmes adored Wagner; he said it helped him to introspect, though I cannot see how this was possible. I loathed that music with a passion. It was all I could do to keep my eyes open and my ears closed as I endeavoured to get through that interminable evening. Holmes, seated on my right, was utterly enrapt with the music from the moment it commenced. He spoke only once, and that was to point out the great Vitelli, a short fellow with an atrocious blond hairpiece and chubby legs, who was engaged in the central part. I can state with certainty that his legs were chubby, because his bearskin costume allowed for a generous view of them. He was indeed past his prime.

"In any case, he should not attempt Wagner," Holmes remarked afterwards. "It is not his *forte*."

Forte or not, prime or not, Holmes was in another world for two solid hours; his eyes were closed much of the time, and his hands waved unobtrusively in his lap to the music, whilst my eyes roved restlessly about the theatre, seeking a respite from the enveloping boredom.

If any person in that place was more wearied by the opera than I, it was Freud. His eyes were closed, not in concentration but in sleep, for which I envied him. Every now and again he would begin to snore, but Frau Freud would nudge him on these occasions and he would awaken with a startled expression, looking about in confusion. Waltzes, and little besides, were the extent of his feeling for music. Holmes's desire to attend the opera had prompted his invitation. No doubt he wished to encourage the first sign of interest in the outside world on the part of his patient. Once here, however, Freud was unable to respond to either the singing or the stage effects, some of which were quite beguiling. He watched dully when a dragon, cleverly simulated by a most complex piece of machinery, appeared at one point and the great Vitelli prepared to slay * it. The dragon, however, began to sing, and that soon sent Freud off to sleep again. It must have had the same effect on me. The next thing I knew the gas was up and people were rising from their seats.

During this first interval I gave my arm to Frau Freud and we four sauntered to the vestibule in search of champagne. As we drew near the overhanging boxes of the first tier, Holmes stopped and looked up at them.

"If Baron Von Leinsdorf patronized the theatre," said he quietly, amidst the throng, "then perhaps he also maintained a box at the opera." He indicated the boxes with a flicker of his eyelids, but did not incline his head.

"Surely," agreed Freud, suppressing a yawn, "but I obtained no definite information on the subject."

"Let us make an effort to find out," Holmes suggested, and moved towards the foyer.

Those aristocratic or wealthy families so fortunate as to possess a box had no need to stand in the press seeking refreshment; liveried attendants kept a special supply on hand for them and brought it right to the box. For the rest of us, it required a combination of ingenuity and daring (as at the old Criterion Bar) to squeeze one's way past an outer

---

* The opera would appear to have been *Siegfried*, though Watson's memory seems to play him false when he attributes the dragon's demise to the first act.

circle of ladies and through an inner congregation of gentlemen, all pounding the bar for service.

Leaving Freud and his wife to chat, Holmes and I volunteered to run this gauntlet, and shortly returned victorious, though indeed, I had spilt most of my own glass when I swerved too late from the path of an energetic young man coming in the opposite direction.

We found Freud talking with a very tall and dandified gentleman who looked younger at first glance than at the second. Fastidiously dressed, he peered at the world through the thickest-lensed pince-nez I think I have ever seen. His features were handsome and regular and exceedingly earnest, though he smiled slightly when Freud introduced us.

"May I present Hugo Von Hofmannsthal. My wife you know, I believe, and these gentlemen are my guests, Herr Holmes and Dr. Watson."

Von Hofmannsthal was obviously surprised.

"Not Herr Sherlock Holmes and Dr. John Watson?" he demanded. "This is indeed an honour!"

"No less for ourselves," Holmes responded smoothly, with an inclination of his head, "if we are addressing the author of *Gestern*."

The grave middle-aged dandy bowed and blushed to the roots of his hair, a reaction of pleased embarrassment I should not have associated with his demeanour. I did not know what this *Gestern* Holmes referred to might be, and so kept tactfully silent.

For some moments we stood in a small knot, idly drinking champagne, whilst Holmes engaged Von Hofmannsthal in an animated discussion of his operas and quizzed him about his collaborator, someone named Richard Strauss, who was, however, no relation that I could determine to the

Strauss of waltz fame.* Our new acquaintance replied as best he could in halting English, and, turning aside Holmes's more complex questions about which poetic metre he preferred to use in comedy, asked about our presence in Vienna.

"Is it that you on a case are here?" he wondered, his eyes bright as a schoolboy's with eagerness.

"Yes and no," Holmes responded. "Tell me," he went on, before the other could pursue the new topic of conversation, "does the new Baron Von Leinsdorf take the same interest in the opera that his father did?"

The question was such an unexpected one that Von Hofmannsthal quite forgot himself for a moment and simply stared at my companion. I understood the logic behind it, however; if Von Hofmannsthal was part of the operatic scene here in Vienna, his knowledge of its patrons would almost certainly be intimate.

"It is strange that you should ask," the poet replied slowly, twirling the stem of his glass absently as he spoke.

"Why strange?" asked Freud, who had been following the exchange with keen interest.

"Because until tonight my answer would have been no." Von Hofmannsthal spoke in rapid but clearly enunciated German. "I have never known him to take any interest in opera at all, and, to be candid, I feared that music in Vienna had lost a powerful benefactor when the old Baron died."

"And now?" Holmes asked.

---

* Holmes's interest in Von Hofmannsthal and familiarity concerning his association with Strauss shows him to have been *au courant* regarding innovative artistic endeavour. Some decades hence these two artists were to overwhelm the world with *Der Rosenkavalier*.

"And now," returned the poet in English, "he comes to the opera."

"He is here tonight?"

Von Hofmannsthal, mystified, and partially convinced that Holmes's question was directly connected with the progress of a case, nodded excitedly.

"Come. I show him to you."

People were now wandering back into the theatre in response to the chimes which announced that the piece was about to resume. Von Hofmannsthal —though he was not sitting in the stalls (and had in fact been fetching champagne for someone who never received it when Freud encountered him)— led us down towards our seats. He then turned and pretended to be looking for someone he knew in the balconies and nudged Holmes gently with his elbow.

"There. Third from the centre on the left."

We looked where he indicated and beheld a box with two figures sitting in it. First glance revealed a sumptuously attired lady with emeralds flashing in her intricately coiffed dark hair. She was seated motionless next to a handsome gentleman who was restlessly surveying the theatre throng with his opera glasses. Beneath them a well-trimmed beard adorned a strong chin and framed thin, sensual lips. Something was disturbingly familiar about that bearded chin, and I fancied for an instant that its owner was looking at us, so ostentatious was Von Hofmannsthal's attempt to be discreet. He was a dramatist, of course, and believed that he was rendering Holmes a service in a criminal investigation (which in fact he was). Yet he allowed himself, I think, to be carried away by the melodramatic properties of the moment, although no doubt he meant well.

Suddenly, the gentleman in the box lowered his opera glasses and Freud and I gasped in chorus.

It was the young villain with the scar whom Freud had trounced on the tennis courts at the Maumberg. If the Baron saw or recognized either of us, he gave no sign, and if Sherlock Holmes was aware of our reactions he too did not change his attitude.

"Who is the lady?" Holmes enquired behind me.

"Ah, that is his step-mother, I believe," said Von Hofmannsthal, "the American heiress Nancy Osborn Slater Von Leinsdorf."

I was still watching that frozen beauty as the house-lights went down, and I felt Holmes tugging at my sleeve, urging me to resume my seat. I did as directed, but reluctantly, and could not resist turning once more to gaze at that strange couple —the handsome young Baron and his chiseled, immobile companion whose emeralds gleamed in the dark from where she sat as the curtain rose on the second act.

12

Revelations

It need hardly be said that whatever interest the second half of the opera held for me, the performance was utterly exploded by Hugo von Hofmannsthal's identification of the woman in Baron Von Leinsdorf's box as his widow! My whirling brain endeavoured to grasp the information and make sense of it. Holmes was of no use at all; I tried to whisper to him during the prelude, but he silenced me with a demure finger on his lips and surrendered himself to the music, leaving me to my own excited speculations.

Here was another set of possibilities. Either the woman was in fact the fabulous widow of the munitions king, or she was an impostor. If she was whom she claimed—and I had certainly to own she looked the part—then who on earth was our client that she should be provided with such intimate information, and as a consequence (no doubt) have been abducted?

I stole a glance at Freud and saw that he, too, was pondering the problem. At first glance he appeared to be interesting himself in the plight of the man in the bearskin, but a flicker of his eyelids betrayed his errant thoughts.

In the landau, as we rode home afterwards, Holmes was of no help, refusing to discuss the matter and confining himself to comments about the performance.

When we had safely settled in the study at Bergasse 19, Freud bade his wife good night and offered us brandy and cigars. I accepted both, but Holmes contented himself with a lump of sugar plucked from the white china bowl in the kitchen. We were settled in our chairs and prepared to discuss our next move when Holmes mumbled an excuse and said he would return in a moment. Freud frowned as he left the room, pursed his lips and eyed me unhappily.

"Would you excuse me, too, doctor? Or perhaps you had best come along."

Mystified, I followed him as he strode rapidly out of the study and fairly raced up the stairs. Without knocking, he burst open the door of Holmes's room. We found him staring at a syringe and a bottle of what I knew to be cocaine, sitting upon the top of the bureau. He did not seem surprised to see us, but I was so startled to discover him in this attitude that I simply gaped at the sight. Freud remained motionless as well. He and Holmes appeared to be holding some form of silent communion. At last, with a short rueful smile, the detective broke the silence.

"I was just considering it," said he, slowly and a trifle mournfully.

"So your lump of sugar informed me," Freud told him. "Some of your methods are not unrelated to medical observations, you know. At any rate, you must ponder well: you cannot be of service to us or to the lady you undertook to help this morning at the hospital if you revert to this practice now."

"I know it."

He stared again at the bottle on the dresser, his chin propped up in his palms. The cocaine and the syringe took on the bizarre aspect of offerings at an altar. I shuddered to think how many wretched folk were forced by their compulsion to view narcotics as a religion and a god, but I knew before Holmes rose and turned away from them that he was no longer of their number.

He scooped up the vial and needle and casually handed them to Freud (I never did learn how or where he had procured them) and, picking up his black briar, followed us out of the room, closing the door softly behind him.

Returning to our chairs in the study, Freud chose not to allude to the incident. Instead, he related our encounter with the young Baron at the Maumberg, a recital to which the detective listened without comment, except to remark, "No backhand? That is interesting. How was his service?"

I interrupted this curious line of enquiry to ask if Holmes had arrived at any conclusions regarding the case.

"Only the obvious ones," he returned, "and they must remain provisional, subject to further data and subsequently to proof."

"How are they distinguished?" Freud demanded.

"In a court of law, I am afraid. We may come to all the conclusions we please, but unless we can prove them we might just as well have remained in bed." He chuckled, and helped himself to the brandy he had declined earlier. "They have been very clever; deuced clever. And where their cleverness has not availed, nature has come to their rescue by presenting us with a witness whose testimony is not only limited but would undoubtedly be suspect if not totally invalid in a court."

He sat in silent thought, puffing at his briar while we watched, neither of us daring to break in upon his reflections.

"I am afraid my grasp of European politics is not particularly profound," he sighed at last. "Dr. Freud, could you assist me?"

"In what way?"

"Oh, just a little general information. Prince Otto Von Bismarck is alive, is he not?"

"I believe so."

"But he is no longer Germany's chancellor?"

Freud stared at him, bewildered.

"Certainly not; not for nearly a year."

"Ah." He lapsed into profound silence once more as Freud and I exchanged mystified glances.

"But, see here, Herr Holmes, what has Von Bismarck to do with——?"

"Is it possible that you do not see?" Holmes sprang to his feet and began pacing the room. "No, no, I suppose not." Then, returning to his chair he said, "A European war is brewing, that much is evident."

We looked at him, thunderstruck.

"A European war?" I gasped.

He nodded and looked about for another match.

"Of monstrous proportions, if I read the signs aright."

"But how can you infer this from what you have seen today?" Freud's tone indicated his gathering doubt concerning the detective's state of mind.

"From the rapport between Baroness Von Leinsdorf and her step-son."

"But I did not observe any particular rapport," I struck in, my own tones echoing those of our host.

"That is because there was none."

He set down his glass and looked at us keenly with his grey eyes.

"Doctor Freud, is there an office of registry in Vienna where wills are on file?"

"Wills? Why, yes, of course."

"Then I should be obliged if you would have the goodness to spend some time there tomorrow morning and tell me who controls the bulk of Baron Von Leinsdorf's estate."

"I have a patient at ten," the doctor protested automatically, but Holmes smiled grimly and held up a hand.

"Will you believe me when I tell you that not one but millions of lives are at stake?"

"Very well. I shall do as you ask. And what will you do?"

"With the help of Dr. Watson I will search for a chink in the armour of our enemies," Holmes responded knocking the ashes from his pipe. "Can our client travel tomorrow, do you think?"

"Travel? How far?"

"Oh, only within the city. I should like her to meet someone."

Freud considered this for some moments.

"I don't see why not," he answered dubiously. "She appears in perfect health aside from her condition and the feebleness imposed by an inadequate diet, and that should be somewhat remedied already."

"Excellent!" Holmes rose, and yawned, tapping his mouth lightly with the back of his hand. "Our day has been long," he observed, "and as the succeeding ones promise to be still longer, I think it time to retire."

Saying which, he bowed and left the room.

"What can it be that he sees in all this?" I wondered aloud.

"I have no idea," Freud sighed. "At any rate, it is time to sleep. I cannot remember being so tired."

I too was exhausted, but my brain kept racing long after my body was still, trying to piece together the puzzle upon which we had stumbled in the course of our visit to this beautiful yet increasingly sinister city. A European war! Millions of lives! Often I had been astonished by my friend's amazing powers, but never had I seen him infer so much on the basis of so little. And, great heavens, what if it should prove true? I do not know how Freud passed that night, but my dreams surpassed my waking fears. The gay and colourful city of Johann Strauss was no longer revolving to the stately strains of his waltzes, but swirling to the shriek of a terrible nightmare.

The next morning we three shared a hasty breakfast before we departed on our separate errands. Holmes ate with an enthusiasm that pronounced his return to health. Freud ate with decision, but his lack of conversation and worried expression proclaimed that he, like me, had spent a restless night.

We were on the point of parting company at the front door when a messenger arrived with a telegram for Sherlock Holmes. He tore open the missive and perused it greedily before tucking it into the pocket of his Inverness, without comment, and signing to the boy that there was no reply.

"Our plans are unchanged," he said and bowed slightly to Freud, ignoring our evident curiosity. The doctor departed with a disgruntled scowl and Holmes turned to me. "And now, my dear Watson, let us be on our way as well."

We proceeded by fiacre directly to the hospital, where a note in Freud's handwriting secured us the custody of the patient. She appeared much improved physically, though she was still appallingly thin and spoke not a word. Accompanying us without resistance, she stepped obediently into the waiting fiacre outside the gate. Holmes had inscribed our destination on his shirt cuff and we started off across the city on our mysterious errand. The precise nature of the errand he was loath to divulge in the presence of our mute passenger, as he indicated when I enquired.

"All in good time, Watson. All in good time."

"What do you expect Dr. Freud to find at the registry?" I asked, determined to be made a party to his plans.

"What I know he will find."

He turned and smiled reassuringly at our client, but she stared straight ahead, seemingly unaware of his gesture, her blue-grey eyes vacantly devoid of expression.

The fiacre crossed the Danube Canal and entered a section of the city occupied by spacious and, in some instances, palatial residences. These were set back some distance from the street and were shielded by high shrubbery from more than a modest view of scalloped towers and imposing grounds.

We stopped at length on Wallenstein Strasse and turned into a wide drive that led to a hideous enough house situated on a slight rise of ground; the area immediately before it was occupied by an elaborate formal garden.

A closed carriage stood beneath the *porte cochère,* and, as we handed down our client, the door to the house opened and out strode a gentleman of medium height with the straightest back I have ever seen. Though he was dressed in a civilian greatcoat and mufti, his movements bore that unmistakable precision one associates not merely with the military but with the strictest Prussian training. His features, however, were not Prussian. Indeed his face, which struck me as vaguely familiar when I saw it, reminded me more of an English clerk's. He wore a pince-nez, neatly trimmed whiskers, and a slightly distracted air, as though he did not know or remember exactly where he was.

He bowed to us, or rather to the lady on my arm, and graciously tipped his bowler, before disappearing into the carriage, which started off without a word of command that I could detect.

Holmes stared at the retreating vehicle for a moment, frowning.

"Do you recall having seen that gentleman recently, Watson?"

"Yes, but I can't for the life of me think where. Holmes, whose house is this?"

He smiled and pulled the bell.

"It is the Vienna residence of Baron Von Leinsdorf," he replied.

"Holmes, this is monstrous!"

"Why so?" Gently he extricated his arm from my impulsive grasp. "The Baron is not here at the moment."

"But if he should return! You've no idea what harm this confrontation might do—" And I gestured obliquely to our mute companion. "Surely you ought to have discussed the matter with Doctor—"

"My dear Watson," he interrupted serenely, "your sentiments do you credit, and, for all I know, your professional judgement as well. Nevertheless, time is of the essence, and, if it is possible, we must force a play. In any event, she does not appear to be reacting to the sight of the house. Who knows? If she does, it may turn out to be just the sort of shock to get her back on her feet."

This last sentence was completed as the huge door swung wide. A liveried servant of impassive

mien wished to know our business. Holmes handed
him his card, and in German that had improved
steadily with his stay in Vienna, begged that he
present it to the lady of the house.

With no change of expression the fellow took the
card and stepped back, allowing the three of us to
wait in a high vaulted antechamber from which we
could see an enormous rectangular entrance hall,
as opulent and hideous as the exterior of the house.
It was panelled with oak and covered with tapestry,
medieval weapons, and gilt-framed portraits whose
subjects I was unable to study from our position in
the vestibule. Dim light filtered down through incongruously small mullioned windows.

"Have you ever seen a more ghastly place?"
Holmes muttered quietly at my elbow. "Just look
at those ceilings!"

"Holmes, I really must protest this procedure.
At least tell me what is going on. Who is to fight
in this awful war?"

"I fear I have not the slightest notion," he answered languidly, still gazing with disapproval at
the rococo wooden carvings above us.

"Then how on earth do you deduce a—"

"Well, surely," he broke in somewhat testily,
"we have here a contest for the possession of an
estate composed of incalculably productive and ex-
tensive munitions works. It is no great matter to
infer—" He broke off, perceiving the butler returning the length of the hall.

"If you will follow me," the man said with a
gesture, "I shall conduct you to the Baroness."

As it fell out, we had need of a guide, for the
place was so vast and labyrinthine that we never
should have located the lady's drawing room without assistance.

It was furnished in a more contemporary vein

than the other rooms we had glimpsed on our way, but in the same atrocious taste, all gaudy pink chintz with yards of lace antimacassars on every article of furniture in sight.

Seated on a divan in the midst of this single-hued profusion—like some graceful bird at the centre of her nest—was the beautiful woman we had glimpsed the previous evening. She rose as we entered and addressed us in American-accented English.

"Mr. Sherlock Holmes, I believe? To what do I owe the—" She broke off suddenly and uttered a cry of recognition, her hand involuntarily flying to her bosom, her magnificent eyes wide with astonishment.

"Good God!" she exclaimed. "Is it Nora?"

She rushed forward, ignoring Holmes and myself, and took the arm of our client, gently leading her to the light, where she peered intently into her face. For her part, our charge remained as pliant yet listless as ever, tolerating the Baroness's scrutiny with what almost appeared to be the weariest indifference.

"What has happened?" that lady cried, glancing from one to the other of us in imperious confusion. "She is very changed."

"You know the lady?" Holmes asked quietly, watching closely as the Baroness returned her attention to the woman she had called Nora.

"Know her? Why, to be sure I know her. This is my personal maid, Nora Simmons. She has been missing for weeks without a trace. Great heavens, Nora, what has happened and how ever did you contrive to reach Vienna?"

Her features were clouded with bewilderment and then with concern as she studied the wan countenance of the other woman.

"I fear you will find her unable to answer your questions," Holmes stated, gently disengaging the ladies and helping Nora Simmons (if that, indeed, was who she was), to a seat. Briefly, he then proceeded to explain to the Baroness how we had chanced upon her servant.

"But this is monstrous!" the lady exclaimed when he had done. "She was abducted, you say?"

"So it would appear," the detective responded in neutral tones. "Do I understand you to say that she accompanied your ladyship to Bavaria?"

"She never left my side from the moment we sailed—except on her days off." The Baroness's complexion mounted to a magnificent hue of indignation as she spoke. "It was under those circumstances that she disappeared some three weeks ago."

"The day of the Baron's death?"

The lady flushed yet more deeply and clasped her hands.

"Why, yes. Nora was not in the villa when the misfortune occurred; she was in the town below us —Ergoldsbach, I believe it is called. In the confusion, she was not missed. In any case, as I have said, it was her day off. When she did not return the following morning I thought that perhaps, having learned of the tragedy, she had, for some reason, fallen into a panic. Hers was an excitable and nervous disposition, as I had good cause to know." She paused. "You see, we were always very close —much more than mistress and maid, really—but when she failed to return and sent no word of farewell, I began to fear something untoward had occurred, and informed the police. Perhaps I should have done so sooner had not my husband's unexpected demise so thrown me into confusion."

"You refer to 'something untoward.' You had no suspicion of foul play?"

"I did not know what to think. She was gone—" the Baroness broke off helplessly, accompanied by a little bird-like gesture. It was easy to see she was overcome not only by the experience but by the mere recollection of it. Nevertheless, Holmes persisted.

"And the police were unable to discover the whereabouts of your maid?"

She shook her head, then impulsively seized the inert hands of the other woman and pressed them with affection.

"Dear girl, how relieved I am to find you!"

"May one enquire in what manner your husband met his death?" Holmes asked, eyeing her intently.

The Baroness coloured violently once more and looked from one to the other of us in considerable confusion.

"His heart," she said simply, in a voice almost too low to carry. I coughed to cover my own confusion, while Holmes rose to his feet.

"I am sorry to hear it. Well, it appears our business here is finished, Watson," said he, easily, and, I thought, with little feeling. "We have solved our little mystery." He held out his hand for Nora Simmons. "Madame, we are sorry to have intruded upon your grief and valuable time."

"But surely you are not taking her from me!" the Baroness cried, rising as well. "I have only just regained her, and I assure you, Mr. Holmes, she is essential to my happiness."

"In her present condition she could hardly be of use to you," Holmes observed drily. "She needs care more than is able to care for others." Again he extended his hand.

"Oh, but I shall care for her myself," the lady

protested emphatically. "Have I not said that she is my companion as well as my servant?" There was something so piteous in her supplications that I was on the point of agreeing with her and professing as much to Holmes, for loving attention can sometimes effect a cure where medicine is helpless. But he spoke abruptly.

"I am afraid such a solution is quite impossible at present, as your maid is under the care of Dr. Sigmund Freud at the Allgemeines Krankenhaus; we have taken a great liberty, as it is, in bringing her to this place without his proper consent. I would not have done so had I not felt an identification was of the utmost moment."

"But—"

"On the other hand, it is just possible that I can persuade the doctor to release the woman into your custody. In Providence you no doubt involved yourself in church work among the destitute and homeless?"

"I was very active in parish work of that sort," the Baroness agreed hastily.

"I thought as much. You may rest assured I will communicate that fact to Dr. Freud and he will no doubt consider it when the time comes to decide upon the proper disposition of his patient."

She would have made reply, but Holmes was smoothly insistent and we took our leave, bearing away with us the unfortunate maid.

Our fiacre was waiting for us where we had left it, and as we climbed inside Holmes allowed himself a fit of silent laughter.

"A very excellent performance, Watson. One in which sheer nerve and ingenuity were matched with the consummate artistry of an Ellen Terry. Of course they were prepared for this sort of eventuality. The woman has been cleverly coached."

"She is an impostor, then?" It seemed almost impossible to believe that magnificent creature a fraud, but Holmes nodded wearily, spilling some charred fragments of tobacco from his pipe as he jerked his head in the direction of our passenger.

"This wretched woman is the *bona fide* Baróness Von Leinsdorf—for all the good it will do her," he added solemnly. "Yet we may, before this business is done, be able to restore some of her rights, if not her sanity."

"How do you know the other is lying?"

"You mean what gave her away—in addition to that preposterous tale of the maid fleeing the house without notice because the master succumbs to heart failure?"

I nodded, and said I had not found the story so very unlikely.

"Perhaps there was some connection between the events of which we are unaware that would help to clarify her actions," I pursued, warming to the theory that had been slowly taking shape in my mind. "Perhaps—"

"Perhaps," he agreed, smiling. "Yet there are certain facts which strongly favour the conclusions I have already drawn."

There was something so convincing about the Baroness in the person of that splendid woman, and something so unlikely about our own demented candidate for that role, and something so irritatingly self-assured about my companion's manner (when less than a week before he himself had been little better than a raving lunatic—whole once more through my own intervention on his behalf), that it nettled me more than it might have six months earlier in London, to hear him speak so condescendingly.

"And what are these facts?" I demanded sceptically.

"It might interest you to know," he answered, handing over the telegram he had received earlier in the day and ignoring the hostile tone in my voice, "that the Slaters of Rhode Island have, for more than two hundred years, belonged to the religious sect known as Quakers. Quakers do not attend church; they go to meeting. And they certainly would not refer to charity work as parish work. No, no, certainly not," he added, turning away to gaze out of the window.

This time I was unable to conceal my surprise, but before I had the chance to articulate it he spoke again, still idly glancing about him: "And, incidentally, I have just recalled where we saw Count Von Schlieffen before."

"Count who?"

"Von Schlieffen; the gentleman who passed us as we came in. His picture appeared * in the *Times* some months ago. Didn't you see it? If my memory serves, he had just been named chief of the German General Staff."

---

* Not in a photograph, of course. In 1891 Count Von Schlieffen's picture appeared in the *Times* as a sketch.

13

Sherlock Holmes
Theorizes

Sherlock Holmes stood upon the burgundy hearth
rug of the study in Bergasse 19 and leaned his
elbows on the mantelpiece behind him.

"The will leaves everything to the new Baroness," said he.

Dr. Freud looked up from his notes with a hurt
expression.

"If you knew the provisions of the Baron's will,
you might have said so," he observed curtly. "As
it is, I have missed a patient on your account, as
I told you I would. Yet you replied that my going
to the registry of wills was of paramount importance."

Holmes laughed in that silent fashion of his and
held up a deprecating hand.

"You will pardon me, I am sure, Doctor. I was
speaking from conviction, not from knowledge.
Your morning has not been wasted: your facts
have confirmed my suspicions. Yet I take my oath;
if my German had been sufficiently fluent, I should
never have prevailed upon you to miss a patient.
Dr. Watson here will tell you it is not my habit to

tear him away from his own practise without good reason. You forgive me? Good!"

So saying, Holmes told Freud of our own excursion. He frowned with disapproval when he learned whither we had taken his patient, but relaxed again when I assured him that neither the house nor its occupants had appeared to make the slightest impression on her.

"The time has now arrived," continued Holmes, fetching forth his disreputable clay—though maintaining his attitude against the mantel—"to marshal our facts and see if they are covered by our theories." He paused to extract a warm coal from the fire with the tongs, and light his pipe. "Let me ask you one final question, however, before I pronounce my case complete. What manner of man is Germany's new Kaiser?"

"He's been Kaiser since 1888," I put in. Holmes nodded but kept his eyes fastened on Freud, who was considering the question with a speculative air.

"If I were forced to use one word, I should refer to him as immature," said he at length.

"What of his policies?"

"They revolve for the most part around social legislation. He is deathly afraid of socialism; and his foreign relations are inclined—so far as I can determine by reading the papers—to truculence, particularly towards Russia, over such issues as property rights in the Balkans."

"His nature?"

"That is more difficult. He is bright, apparently, but excitable, given to fits of impatience with those around him. I believe it was one of those conflicts that resulted in the dismissal of Prince Von Bismarck. The Kaiser is fond of military displays—of uniforms, parades, and demonstrations of personal power. He—" Freud hesitated with a short laugh.

"Yes?"

"Actually, I have had a theory about the Kaiser for some time now."

"I should be most interested in hearing it," Holmes offered politely, without hesitation.

"It is hardly subtle." Freud rose brusquely to his feet as though annoyed with himself for having mentioned the theory.

"Pray allow me to judge its relevance to my case," Holmes insisted, pressing his finger-tips together and leaning back against the mantel, the pipe clenched between his teeth and smoke curling upwards in a steady spiral.

Freud shrugged.

"You may have known—either from seeing pictures of him or from reading on the subject—that the Kaiser possesses a withered arm."

"A withered arm?"

"The result of some childhood disease—possibly poliomyelitis. I am not certain. In any case, physically he is not a complete man." Here Freud paused and eyed me askance. "You are the first to hear this peculiar notion of mine."

Holmes regarded him behind the pipe smoke.

"Go on."

"Well—briefly—it has occurred to me that perhaps the Kaiser's insistent emphasis on displays of strength, his love of colourful uniforms—particularly those with cloaks which manage to conceal his deformity—the parades, the medals with which he adorns himself—it has occurred to me that these bellicose loves are all in some way manifestations of his feelings of personal inadequacy. They might all be construed as elaborate compensations for the withered arm. An ordinary cripple need not feel so sensitive as he, moreover, for he is the king and descendant of a long line of conspicuously noble and heroic ancestors."

I was so utterly absorbed in the doctor's statement that I forgot Holmes was in the room. When Freud had finished, I shifted my gaze and saw that Holmes was regarding him with fixed attention and wonder in his expression. Slowly, Holmes sank into the chair opposite mine.

"This is most remarkable," said he, finally. "Do you know what you have done? You have succeeded in taking my methods—observation and inference—and applied them to the inside of a subject's head."

"Scarcely a subject." Freud smiled shortly. "In any event your methods—as you refer to them— are not covered by a patent, I trust?" His tone was mild, yet the satisfaction in it was evident. Like Holmes, he was not without vanity. "Yet what I have surmised may prove totally erroneous. You yourself have noted the dangers of reasoning with insufficient data at one's disposal."

"Remarkable," Holmes echoed. "Not only does it possess the ring of truth—or of plausibility, if you prefer—it also conforms to certain facts and theories I shall now lay before you." He got to his feet once more, but paused, distracted, before commencing. "Remarkable. You know, Doctor, I shouldn't be surprised if your application of my methods proves in the long run far more important than the mechanical uses I make of them. But always remember the physical details. No matter how far into the mind you may travel, they are of supreme importance."

Sigmund Freud nodded and bowed, slightly overcome, I think, by the detective's abrupt and effusive praise.

"Now, then," Holmes resumed, his thoughts col-

lected, "let me tell you a story." He relit his pipe
as the doctor settled himself into an attitude of
attention. Like the detective, Sigmund Freud was a
great listener, though indeed the two men showed
their absorption in a client's statement in entirely
different fashions. Freud did not listen with his eyes
closed and his finger-tips pressed together. On the
contrary, he leaned his bearded cheek on an open
palm, propped his elbow on the arm of his chair,
threw one leg across the other, and watched whoever was speaking with wide, sad, steadfast eyes.
Even the cigar which he held in his other hand
could not make him squint with its pungent smoke.
At such times he gave the impression of peering
directly into one's soul, an impression that Holmes,
a sensitive observer, could not fail to grasp, as he
launched into his story.

"A wealthy widower with an only son he does
not care for particularly—and who does not care
for him—goes travelling to the United States. There
he meets a young woman half his age, yet in spite
of this disparity (or perhaps because of it), they
fall in love. Knowing that his own years are numbered, they are married without delay. The woman
comes from a well-to-do Quaker background and
the two are joined together in a Quaker church,
known as a 'meeting house.' This phrase, later mumbled by our client, was understood as 'meat-house,'
and in that connexion mistakenly associated itself
with our hypothetical warehouse and literally put
us off the scent for a time.

"The couple returns to the isolated home of the
husband in Bavaria, where the first thing the bride-
groom does is to alter his will in favour of his bride.
Her religious views on the subject, as well as his
own convictions, advancing with the years, make
it impossible for him to retain control of an empire

dedicated to the manufacture of war matériel. Having neither the strength nor the inclination to devote his last years to the dismantling of his factories, he very simply puts the entire matter into her hands in the event of his death, to do with as she sees fit.

"The old gentleman, however, has not reckoned with—or has badly under-estimated—the wrath of his prodigal son. Finding his hopes cut off, cut off literally from untold millions, this young devil proves capable of drastic steps to regain them. Politically conservative himself, and raised in the New Germany, he possesses certain connexions and he uses them. Offers are made to certain people, people who have no intention of allowing a foreign commoner—much less a woman!—to dismantle the core of the Kaiser's war machine. The young man is given *carte blanche,* and is no doubt assigned some help. We have yet to discover how it was managed, but he somehow accomplishes the death of his father—"

"Holmes!"

"And then proceeds to spirit his step-mother out of Germany and into a warehouse prison near the Danube Canal, here in Vienna. The father's will is on file in the two countries where he holds property, and the bride is now urged to sign over her interest to the son. This she courageously refuses to do. Her love and her religious convictions lend her a strength that resists starvation, and all manner of threats besides. In her lonely confinement, her mind begins to give way. Ingeniously, she manages to escape. Only when she is free, however, is the utter hopelessness of her situation borne in upon her. She speaks no German, knows no one, and is too weak to take the initiative. The bridge is the nearest and simplest solution, but passing constables prevent it, at which point she retreats into the helpless state that you, Doctor, have already described so well."

He paused and took several rapid puffs of his pipe, tactfully allowing us the time to digest his reasoning thus far.

"What of the lady we saw at the opera?" Freud wondered, sitting back thoughtfully and blowing forth smoke from his cigar.

"The young man we are playing against is as bold as he is cunning. Upon learning that his step-mother has flown her prison, he makes a quick decision. Realizing her position of helplessness as clearly as she, he elects to ignore her. Let her tell her story to whoever can understand her—the thought must have amused him—he would not make himself conspicuous by searching for her or by employing others to do so. He would hire someone to assume her place and bluff through the business of the will with a simple forged signature; for who, when all was said and done, would care to contest the widow's decision? I do not know where he discovered his clever pupil; possibly she is the very maid she pretended to recognize, or else, perhaps, some American actress down on her luck and stranded far from home. But, whoever she is, she has been coached well, and paid well, too, no doubt.

"Foreseeing the slim possibility that his step-mother would be discovered, he even provided her substitute with a convincing story. Of course he must have known his step-mother had lost her wits before her escape. He was confident her mind would not soon be whole enough to command anyone's serious attention. You will recall, Watson, that the woman we spoke with today referred to her maid as Nora Simmons. This is a rather ingenious touch on the part of the young Baron, though as a precaution it was sufficiently *outré* to first arouse my suspicions. That the maid should bear the same initials as the mistress would be a senseless coincidence—unless, of course, some of the clothing she wore during her captivity and escape bore the initials of Nancy Slater. He might better perhaps have said that she departed from the house with some of her mistress's clothing," he continued in a ruminative fashion, sorting out the alternatives as he spoke. "But no. Obviously he had not told that part of the story to the Bavarian police."

"Then the maid's flight was reported the night of the Baron's death?" I asked.

"Or the morning after. It would not surprise me to learn that it was," my friend returned. "The young man with whom we are dealing has, I suspect, learned to play cards from the Americans."

"Meaning?"

"That he always has an ace up his sleeve. The question now—" He was interrupted by a knock on the study door. Paula opened it part-way to announce that an orderly from the Allgemeines Krankenhaus had arrived with a message for Dr. Freud.

No sooner had she uttered these words, than Sherlock Holmes leapt forward with a cry, clapping a hand to his forehead.

"They've taken her!" he yelled. "Fool that I am to have thought they would hesitate, whilst I stood babbling here." He dashed from the room, squeezing past the astonished maid without ceremony, and accosted the unsuspecting orderly in the vestibule, both hands grasping the man's lapels.

"She's gone, is she? Dr. Freud's patient is gone?"

The man nodded dumbly, too startled to reply. He had only been sent on an errand and had no notion of its gravity. He bore a curt note from

Dr. Schultz, wondering what had become of the woman since she had been left in Dr. Freud's hands, and protesting her unorthodox removal from hospital during the afternoon—before he had a chance to see for himself how she was getting on and to conduct an examination prior to her release. In an oblique allusion, Schultz promised to mention the matter to Meynert.

"Were you there when she was carried off?" Holmes demanded of the orderly as he hastily slid into his Norfolk and threw on his Inverness. The man shook his head and said he had not been.

"Then you shall take us round to whoever *was* on duty," the detective informed him briskly, clapping his ear-flapped travelling cap on his head. "Hurry, gentlemen," he called over his shoulder, "we have not a moment to lose. For though we may have nothing so much as a deranged woman at one end of our trail, there lurks a European conflagration at the other!"

14

We Join a Funeral

The cab darted through the late afternoon traffic on its way back to the hospital. No one spoke, except that Holmes continually enjoined the driver to hurry. Each was occupied with his own thoughts. The orderly looked from one to the other of us, wondering, I could tell, what the devil was going on, and wincing as our vehicle dashed in front of street-cars and forced peddlars to leap astride the kerbs and out of our way. Sigmund Freud's large brow was furrowed with thought, while Holmes sat, bent forward, in moody and depressed silence, rousing himself every thirty seconds or so to encourage the driver.

At one point we were forced to come to a complete stop. The street was barred by a troop of Hungarian Life Guards on their way to their posts at the Hofburg. Holmes surveyed the obstacle gloomily, then sat back with a sigh.

"It's no use," he announced abruptly, "she is lost and we are beaten." He ground his teeth with vexation, his grey eyes bright with pain.

"Why so?" Freud asked.

"Because he will kill her the first chance he gets." He pulled out his watch and stared at it mournfully, while from the corner of my eye I beheld the orderly's eyes grow wide with alarm. "And they have had their chance by now. Watson," he said, turning to me, "you would have done better to leave me to the cocaine. I have out-lived my usefulness."

"Permit me to disagree with you on both counts," Freud responded before I could answer, "but I do not think the lady's life is in danger. Drive on, cabbie!" he called to the man as the Life Guards finished obstructing our way. Holmes looked at him briefly, but said nothing as the cab rolled forward and gathered speed.

"You must permit me to do some inferring of my own," Freud pursued, deciding that he must speak without encouragement. "Using the same methods I applied to the Kaiser's personality, I conclude that the Baroness may be in grave peril, but I cannot believe that her step-son plans to murder her now that she is in his hands once more."

"Why not?" Holmes countered without real interest. "It would be the most practical move he could make."

"It would have been more practical still if he had disposed of her at the same time he arranged the death of his father, wouldn't you say?"

The question captured Holmes's attention, and he turned to face the doctor directly. Dr. Freud seized his opportunity, and went on.

"Surely, that would have been the simplest solution. Arrange matters so that both are killed in an accident and then he inherits the entire estate automatically. So runs the will, and he must have known it."

Holmes frowned.

"Why didn't he?" he wondered aloud.

"Would you care to hear my theory?"

Holmes nodded, his eyes alive with interest at the slim possibility of hope the doctor held out.

"It will take too long to detail my researches," Freud began, "but it is my opinion that the young man in question hates his step-mother with a passion that far exceeds the impediment she represents to his political or financial schemes."

"Why so?" I interrupted, in spite of myself. "He can scarcely know her, and if that is the case, how has he developed the hatred you postulate?"

Freud turned to me.

"But you do admit that his behaviour towards his step-mother has been hateful?"

"Oh, quite."

"So hateful—" The cab lurched to one side, momentarily interrupting Freud as we braced ourselves.

"So hateful, in fact, that though it would have been infinitely simpler to dispose of her, he yet preferred to keep her alive, fraught with peril though such a decision has proved to be, in order to imprison and torture her past bearing and past sense."

Holmes nodded, pursing his lips as he considered the situation thus outlined.

"Therefore," Freud continued, as we drew near the hospital, "using your own methods, we must infer another motive. What would you say if I told you this fanatical hatred existed before he ever met the woman his father had married, and would have existed no matter whom he had wed?"

"What?"

"You see, the young man's extraordinary behaviour towards the step-mother he does not know can only be explained in one fashion. And that is

189

that he is so loyal and devoted to the memory of his true mother that his father's action and this woman's consent have outraged the most elemental depths of his character. For the father's betrayal of his first wife: instant death. For the false mother: lingering survival—even though it is impractical from other points of view. That is the only theory that covers all the facts, and as you have yourself observed upon occasion, Herr Holmes, when the probable has been excluded, the remainder, however strange, must be the truth. I have applied your methods correctly, have I not? And if so, we may depend upon it, the woman is still alive, however menaced. Here we are."

Holmes stared at him for a half second before springing out and rushing towards the gate, pulling the orderly by the hand. Dr. Freud and I followed, instructing the driver to wait.

Inside, we were led without delay to the porter who had released Freud's patient earlier in the day. The porter spoke with exasperating precision, pompously interjecting his sentiments regarding the irregularity of procedure surrounding the patient's departure.

"Imagine every inmate released by a note without a proper—" Holmes broke in without ceremony.

"Describe the people who fetched her, if you please," said he curtly, whereat the fellow turned slowly round and scrutinized him. From his manner and from my companion's breathless posture—and his foreign-looking costume—it was evident to me that the porter took him for a potential resident in the Psychiatric Ward.

"Please hurry!" I pleaded, seeing that he made no move to speak. "It is of the utmost importance."

"Describe them?" the stupid fellow repeated slowly. "Why I'm hanged if I can describe 'em. You knew who they were, didn't you?" he turned to Dr. Freud.

"I?" Freud echoed, astonished. "If I knew them, why should I be asking you for a description?"

"But—" spluttered that frustrating individual, "they said they had been sent by you!" And he looked at Freud as though he, too, might be a candidate for permanent residency.

For a moment we stared at each other blankly. Then Holmes broke into a dry chuckle of appreciation.

"Cunning and nerve!" he exclaimed, shaking his head. "My statement to the lady at Wallenstein Strasse this morning put the idea into their heads, as well as telling them where the fugitive was to be found. Now, my man, give us a description."

"Well—" The porter launched into a vague memory of two men, one short, choleric, and shifty-eyed, the other tall, dignified, and impassive.

"That will be the butler," Holmes interposed. "Doctor," he said, turning to Freud, "you had best leave word here to send for the police. We shall want them before this business is done. Tell them that a woman has been abducted from this hospital and leave the Wallenstein Strasse address. We shall go there now."

Freud nodded, and was about to repeat the message to the porter when Fate played into our hands, for once, in the person of Dr. Schultz, who was striding rapidly towards us.

"Ah, Dr. Freud," he commenced sententiously, "I've been meaning to have a word with you—"

"And I with you," Freud interrupted, and told him what had happened, omitting, as Holmes had suggested, some of the improbable though crucial details. He identified the Baroness in the character of the maid, and said she had been kidnapped.

"Send the police as quickly as possible," he enjoined the startled surgeon, scribbling the Von Leinsdorf address in the margin of the porter's register.

Without pausing for reply, we three dashed off for our cab and bounded in.

"Seventy-six Wallenstein Strasse!" Holmes yelled, "and hurry as you value your life!"

The man muttered something about going at a sane pace as he valued his life, but snapped the reins and we were off once again. If there had been space, I believe Holmes would have paced within that cab; as it was, the confines prevented him from doing more than gnaw at his knuckles.

"You have your revolver, Watson?" he asked me. I assured him that I had thought to thrust it into my ulster on our way out. He nodded approvingly. "Of course, he has reckoned without Dr. Freud's reasoning, which means that he believes himself secure. He assumes we believe he will murder the woman at his first opportunity and dispose of the body. He may not even suspect we are on his track—" But he did not sound like a man convinced, and trailed off, his knuckles crammed against his teeth again.

"Will he be so foolish?" I wondered, taking up the thread. "Surely we shall not find her at the villa."

"I fear not," he acknowledged grudgingly, "but where, *where* will he take her?" He pondered another moment in silence. "He knows the alarm will be given, whether or not we pursue him directly, that much is certain. He will be questioned, if he—" He trailed off once more, and I knew from past experience that he was now trying to place himself in the position of the cunning young baron, and, using the portrait so ably painted for him by

Freud, decide what his next move would be had Fate cast him in the role of that maniacal nobleman.

We pulled into the drive of 76 Wallenstein Strasse, our horses streaming with foam, to find the Viennese Constabulary aimlessly patrolling the grounds. Dr. Schultz's telephone call had alerted them and they had arrived by motor launch. A tall, straight sergeant, with white-blond hair and alert blue eyes, was in command. He strolled quickly over as we debarked and addressed my friend with a rigid salute.

"Herr Holmes? We have just arrived, but the house is closed and no one appears within." His English was studied but serviceable.

"As I surmised," the detective responded with a disconsolate sigh. "We are too late." He glanced about moodily.

"This is not a reflection on us, I hope," the sergeant said anxiously. "We got here so soon as we were notified."

"No, no, the fault is none of yours, though your men have made a fine mess of the ground. It could not be worse if a troop of Uhlan had passed over it. Still, we may as well have a look." So saying, he started up the slope towards the house, the eager sergeant at his elbow.

"Herr Holmes, your reputation is well-known to us and the prefect has ordered me to place my men at your disposal."

"Really?" Holmes stopped, impressed. "It's a pity they don't share your prefect's views at the Yard," he added, and began walking again, his eyes fixed on the muddied lawn before him. I heard him mutter something about how it was hard that no prophet was ever regarded as such in his own land.

Freud made as if to follow, but I laid a restraining hand upon his arm and explained in low tones that at such times we should only be in Holmes's way. He nodded and remained where he stood.

Holmes's survey of the house was confined to a hasty examination of the area by the *porte cochère,* during which he trotted back and forth, sometimes in circles, uttering little yelps and whines of satisfaction, curiosity, or displeasure. At such moments his resemblance to a hound was most remarkable; his keen features, particularly the aquiline nose, the slung-forward posture of his body, and the shambling gait, all tended to suggest some dog intent on picking up the scent of its prey. But for the magnifying glass which he now whipped out and used to examine the earth, he would have reminded me very much of Toby, casting anxiously about for a lead.

Dr. Freud, the sergeant, and the police watched this performance with differing expressions of incredulity upon their faces; Freud with the absorption in all facets of Holmes that was characteristic of him thus far; the sergeant with dubious professional interest, as one who seeks to learn from a master but who cannot quite bring himself to believe that such bizarre behaviour is meant to do anything but impress observers; his subordinates with open smiles of scepticism. If they knew of Holmes, they knew by hear-say only, and this demonstration meant nothing to them whatever. They suspected it was mere affectation. I could have told them otherwise; that Holmes was capable of extremely affected behaviour on occasion, but that this was assuredly not one of those occasions.

Suddenly he halted, his body quivering over some detail in the ground. He threw himself down upon his face and remained there for some moments, then rose to his full height and rapidly descended the knoll.

"There is every indication they have placed the woman inside a large steamer trunk and are carrying her with them out of the country."

The sergeant was too dumb-founded to speak, so astonished was he by Holmes's methods, but I, who was more familiar with their reputation for accuracy, did not question them.

"But Holmes, where he is taking her?"

"Where?" He thought for a moment, then snapped his fingers. "Why to Bavaria, of course! Once he crosses the border he will be as safe as the Emperor in Schönbrunn. Blast!" This was in reference to the spent horses belonging to our cab.

"Come on, Watson!" he called, running down the drive. "We must find other transportation to the nearest terminus!"

Freud, the sergeant, and I—followed at the heels by the confused constables—raced out past the front gate in Holmes's wake and into the placid street.

We almost collided with him around the corner beyond the gate, for he had skidded to a stop, his Inverness flapping wildly about him. At the far end of the street, entering it at an appropriate pace, was an ornate funeral procession—the hearse, the horses, the carriages, and many pedestrian mourners all dressed in obsequious black. Obviously, the demise of some peer or merchant prince had occasioned this awful display of solemnity, but Holmes's eye gleamed as he beheld the lugubrious sight and he sprang forward.

"Holmes!"

He paid us no heed. With the constables, Dr. Freud, and me behind, he sprinted towards a huge dark carriage travelling immediately after the hearse. No doubt it contained the corpse's devastated kinsmen, dukes and marquesses all, but Holmes did not hesitate: he threw himself into the box and seized the reins from the astonished coachman, turning the vehicle out of its place in the procession and cracking the whip.

"Watson!"

The carriage thundered towards us and Holmes waved me aboard. As the vehicle raced by, Freud and the stalwart sergeant and I all managed to find something to cling to, and we hauled ourselves up.

It is not possible to do justice to the expressions of surprise and alarm upon the faces of the occupants within. There were four of them, all dressed in consistent and elegant black: a corpulent gentleman with ruddy complexion and white side-whiskers, whose great size dated from an earlier fashion, was spluttering helplessly; a young girl of sixteen or so, her features partially concealed by a veil, stared at us with wide-eyed wonder behind it; an elderly lady, similarly attired and also corpulent, was so engrossed by her grief that I do not think she noticed our presence at all, but continued to sob copious tears into a tiny black cambric handkerchief. Next to her, attempting both to console the woman and to fathom our presence in the carriage, was a young man I put down as a nephew or a son. Torn between filial duty and perplexity, I judged his effectiveness as opponent or as comforter was problematical at best.

I saw all this in a fraction of the time it takes to relate it. I was busy holding onto and opening the door, and handing up my service revolver to Holmes, that he might prevent the coachman's attempting any mischief.

The sergeant had jumped in on the other side and held his own pistol at the ready, though none of the passengers seemed disposed to interfere, nor did they react when he tried—in his most official tones—to assure them that this was an emergency and that there was no cause for alarm. No doubt the statement struck them as contradictory.

There being no more room in the coach, Dr. Freud was obliged to stand on the running-board and cling to the window frame for support, his hair flying in the wind.

The rest of the police and mourners were left behind, utterly.

"Which way is the nearest station?" Holmes called down to the sergeant through the trap.

"The Munich train only goes from—"

"Devil take the Munich train! The nearest station, man!"

The sergeant bawled out directions that would get us to the Heiligenstadt *Bahnhof,* and I could hear Holmes cracking the whip once more above me as we hurtled off in search of it.

Except for the noise of the horses and the creaking of tackle and the sobbing of the elderly lady, no one spoke. The sergeant, whose eyes were roving about the interior of the coach, nudged me and jerked his head in the direction he wished me to look. On the inside panel of the door was an elaborate coat-of-arms.

"I hope Herr Holmes knows what he is doing," he remarked under his breath.

"So do I," was Freud's only comment. His head was in the window and the crest on the opposite panel had also engaged his attention.

"Don't worry," I replied, but the suggestion struck me as idiotic under the circumstances and I regretted having uttered it.

After re-crossing the canal, the coach screeched around a sharp right-hand turn, almost—it seemed to me—lifting two of its wheels off the ground in the process. On the left side, as the carriage regained its equilibrium, I could see massive railway yards, and I assumed we were headed for their terminus at the farther end.

This indeed proved to be the case. Some minutes later the coach jerked to a halt and, before we had dismounted, Holmes was on the ground and running towards the building. As we tumbled after him the sergeant again apologized to the surprised party in the coach for our ghastly intrusion on their occasion of grief, and even offered them a crisp salute, in deference to their exalted rank.

We caught up with Holmes, who was already in excited conversation with the stationmaster, having ascertained that Baron Von Leinsdorf had commissioned a special some three hours before.

"We will also commission a special," Holmes informed him, but the man explained that it required some hours' notice to clear the tracks ahead by telegraph and put together such a train. The Baron had evidently ordered his the moment we had left his house at mid-day.

Holmes listened with half an ear while the good man detailed the difficulties involved, his eyes roaming about the platforms until at last they lighted on an engine and a tender with steam already up and one car behind.

"So you see, *mein Herr*—"

"I'm afraid I haven't time to argue," Holmes interrupted, fetching forth my revolver and showing it to him. "We'll have that one right there, if you don't mind." He jerked the weapon in the direction of the engine.

The man was too amazed to react, but the sergeant, gasping for breath, seemed to feel that things had gone too far.

"Now see here—" he began, but my friend was in no mood for conversation.

"Telegraph the frontier," he ordered. "Tell them to stop that train at all costs. Have them use whatever pretext is necessary and search the trunks. The trunks! Hurry, man, every instant is precious. A woman's life and the course of history may depend on your speed!"

The sergeant's training had not equipped him to resist commands so briskly uttered, and he dashed off to execute them without further remonstrance.

"You will be kind enough to accompany us," Holmes informed the stationmaster, and that unhappy individual shrugged and did as he was bid. The engineer was adjusting valves when we approached, but the situation was soon made clear to him. He raised his eyebrows when the stationmaster informed him that his small train was now a special, but prepared to back out of the station.

"Where are we going?" he demanded, seeing that the stationmaster made no move to leave the train.

"Munich," Holmes told him, displaying the revolver. "Doctor," he turned to Freud before the engineer could make reply, "there is no need for you to go with us. Would you sooner depart?"

Sigmund Freud smiled ruefully and shook his head.

"I have seen too much of this affair to lose sight of it now," he answered, like the stout-hearted fellow he was, "and I have my own score to settle with the Baron. Besides, that woman is my patient."

"Excellent. Now——"

"But we haven't enough fuel for Munich!" the engineer protested, after a delayed response to the revolver and our destination, "and the points—the points are all wrong!"

"We will cross the first obstacle when necessity compels us to," I replied. "And as for the second, we will switch the points as we go."

"I never get your limits, Watson." Holmes smiled thinly. "Off we go then—full speed, mind."

The engineer and stationmaster regarded one another helplessly. The stationmaster nodded with resignation, the engineer heaved a pessimistic sigh and swung round a wheel, and we were off.

15

Pursuit!

Of course it was not possible to proceed at full speed—not getting out of Vienna, at any rate. There were too many points to be switched over, and the track, which ran around the outskirts of the city to the north-west, was not designed for rapid traffic. The first half-hour was quite maddening, therefore, as Dr. Freud and I were constantly obliged to leap from the cab and rush over to change an interminable series of points at the direction of the engineer, whilst Holmes, holding my revolver, saw to it that neither the engineer nor the stationmaster attempted to interfere with our plans.

Night was falling rapidly, which made our task the more difficult. The points were hard to distinguish, and, what was more, we were obliged for safety's sake to change them back again after the train had passed, that no accidents might transpire in our wake.

It would be ironic, indeed, as Holmes pointed out, should our efforts to rescue one woman result in the death of hundreds.

In addition, the points themselves were stiff and

it required the strength of two men—on some of them—to change them over. I was grateful that Freud had elected to accompany us. Without his presence our situation would have proved intolerable.

We worked our way past the Hermalser Park, which, by this time, I was unable to see, and headed south, where we joined the main line leading west from the large terminus where Holmes and I had first arrived in the city what seemed an eon ago. There were endless points to be thrown back and then forth again, and Freud and I were perspiring freely by the time the last one had been accomplished and we were well and truly gaining momentum as we charged into the night.

By this time Holmes had explained the situation to the engineer and the stationmaster, and their attitude underwent a marked change. Instead of working under the threat of a revolver—which Holmes nevertheless retained in his pocket, lest their sentiments change again—they offered to cooperate to the limit of their capabilities.

The night air was chilly as we sped along, but there was work to be done that helped us to stay warm. Those who have never engaged in it cannot fully grasp the exhausting nature of coal shovelling. Yet if we were to maintain the speed essential to overtake the Baron's train it was necessary to pack that engine's furnace with fuel.

And pack it we did! As towns and fields flitted by in the blackness, Freud and I shovelled coal as though our lives depended on it. I was the first to give out. The wound in my leg had grown increasingly painful during all those occasions when Freud and I had jumped on and off the train in order to change the points. At the time, in my state of excitement and exasperation, I had not noticed it but now the leg throbbed with alarming regularity. I was all too aware of the Jezail bullet that had passed through it so many years before, when, during my service in Afghanistan, I had been struck at the battle of Maiwand.

I stoked as far as Neulengbach, where I had to give it up and Holmes took over. He surrendered the weapon to me and I collapsed on the floor of the cab with my back propped against one of the iron sides, nursing my leg but keeping the gun within easy reach. I felt the night wind in earnest now and commenced shivering, though I clenched my teeth and determined to say nothing about it. My friends had their hands full, as it was.

Holmes noticed me, however, as he turned from the boiler with an empty shovel. Without a word he set down the tool, undid his Inverness, and threw it over me. There was no time to speak. My eyes merely flickered in gratitude and he nodded briefly and gave my shoulder a reassuring squeeze before returning to the work.

It was a sight I shall not soon forget—the world's greatest detective and the founding father of that branch of medicine known today as psycho-analysis, side by side in their shirt-sleeves, piling coal into that boiler as though it was work for which they had been born.

Freud, however, was losing strength rapidly. He had done as much as I, and though he had no wound to hamper him, it was nevertheless clear that he was unused to such exertions.

Holmes perceived his plight and ordered him to stop, telling the stationmaster we should be obliged if he would take the doctor's place. The man said he would be happy to work and reached for the shovel. (Had not the space between the engine and the tender been so slight, he would doubtless have assisted us earlier but there was room for only two stokers at the most.)

Freud refused to relinquish the shovel, maintaining that he was yet fit, but Holmes insisted, pointing out that if he got no rest now, he would be unable to relieve anyone later. The argument continued as we passed through Boheimkirchen, whose sign caught my eye momentarily, but the doctor at length relented and surrendered the shovel to the stationmaster, who went to work with a will.

Freud resumed his jacket with a sigh and sat down opposite to me in the cab.

"Cigar?" he shouted.

He held one out to me and I accepted it gratefully. Freud smoked excellent cigars and he smoked them incessantly, much the way Holmes consumed pipes, though, as I have noted, Holmes was less than particular about his tobacco—with predictable olfactory results.

Freud and I smoked in silence. Holmes and the stationmaster continued heaping coal into the boiler, whilst the engineer kept watch on the pressure gauges, the governors, and the track ahead, his worried expression proclaiming his misgivings about the manner in which his locomotive was being handled. At one point he turned back from a brief examination of a gauge and called to the stokers to slow down.

"She'll burst if you don't!" he protested above the din.

"She will not!" the stationmaster retorted angrily. "Pay no attention to him, Herr Holmes. I was driving these engines when he was in knee-pants. Burst, indeed!" he swore, throwing a heaping shovelful into the bowels of the machine. "Why this engine was built by Von Leinsdorf, and who ever heard of a Von Leinsdorf boiler going, *ever?* Ha! Don't mind him, Herr Holmes. It's the younger generation: no courage, no daring—and no respect for their elders!" he concluded with a backward sweep of his hand in the direction of the timid engineer.

"One moment," Holmes interrupted. "Do you mean to tell me this engine was manufactured by Baron Von Leinsdorf's company?"

"Yes, sir. Yes, indeed! You see the plate?" He heaved another shovelful into the boiler fires, which were glowing white through the door and providing some welcome heat for the cab, and then scraped at a grimy plaque above my head with his sooty handkerchief.

"You see?" he yelled.

Holmes regarded the plaque curiously and drew back with a smile on his face.

"What is it, Herr Holmes?"

"Irony, my friend. Irony. Come, keep working!"

And so we thundered on through the night. The stationmaster informed us that the Baron's train consisted of three cars as opposed to our one, and that his locomotive, retained at only a few hours' notice, was not so large or powerful as our own. These facts buoyed our spirits as we whizzed through the sizable town of St. Polten, where there was one set of points to be changed, and Melk, which we rushed past at a speed I dared not guess.

"We must make a decision," the stationmaster shouted above the roar of the engine, as we left Melk behind. "Do you want to go through Linz, or not?"

"What are the alternatives?" Holmes enquired, speaking into the stationmaster's cupped ear.

"Well, if you go through Linz, you will be taking the shorter route to Salzburg," the worthy man informed us, now cupping his hands over his mouth to make himself heard, "but Linz itself will slow you down. There are many points to be changed. If we go south, on the other hand, we pass through Amstetten and Steyr, but they are easier, with fewer points and fewer railroad people to see you do it. But you must make up your mind before we reach Pöchlarn. Also, the track may not be as good in the south," he added as an afterthought.

"But is it usable?"

The stationmaster turned to the engineer, who shrugged and nodded. Holmes looked down at Dr. Freud and me, his face a question.

"How do we know the Baron is going through Salzburg?" Freud inquired. "Perhaps he is headed for Braunau."

"No, that I can promise you," the man answered. "When a special is arranged, the route is chosen and the points are signalled by telegraph, ahead of the train. I cleared the tracks for the Baron myself and I know what route he has chosen."

"That is most fortuitous," Holmes broke in. "What do you recommend?"

The stationmaster thought for a moment, pulling at his moustache and dirtying it with coal dust.

"Go south."

"Very well."

And so it was that we slowed down at the little town of Pöchlarn and Holmes himself descended the train and switched the points.

Dr. Freud and I, rested from our labours, were now in a position to renew them, and did so as we sped towards Amstetten. At the time, I noticed that our coal supply was giving out rapidly, and I said as much to Holmes when I returned to the cab with a load, leaving Freud inside the tender, scraping the remainder of our fuel towards the front. He nodded but said nothing, being in the act of shielding a vesta from the wind as he attempted to light his pipe.

"How much have we left?" he demanded of the stationmaster when this had been accomplished. The man returned with me to the tender, then inspected the gauges presided over by the engineer.

"If we make it to Steyr we'll be lucky."

Holmes nodded once more, got to his feet and, grasping the iron rails on the edge of the tender, hauled himself down the outside of it towards the lone car we were pulling behind. I stopped shovelling and involuntarily held my breath, praying that our speed would not cause him to lose his grip and be swept over the side. His cloak, which he had resumed, was billowing about him like a sail, and the wind blew so strong that it made off with his ear-flapped travelling cap.

He disappeared from view for some time and I went back to shovelling the remainder of our fuel with Freud, but his continued absence worried me. I was on the point of saying so to the doctor, when Holmes climbed into the tender from the rear, throwing before him a pile of curtains and other flammable material from the interior of the car.

"Work on these," he instructed. "I'll be back with more." Saying which, he climbed out of the tender again.

It might be instructive—and even amusing—to detail the manner in which we tore apart that unfortunate car and burned it piece by piece, chair by chair, window frame by window frame, door by door. I say it might prove instructive, but the moment is scarcely appropriate for such a digression.

Suffice it to say that we all took turns, except the engineer, who refused to collaborate and informed us bleakly that we were destroying railway property. The stationmaster favoured him with an oath in German, whose import I was unable to decipher save that it was connected in some way with the man's mother and sounded singularly effective in that language, and then removed an axe from its niche above the plaque and went to work on the carriage himself, by way of example.

As we tore through the night on our mad chase, that car disappeared entirely under our ministrations, and our speed did not slacken. We stopped only to change points in order to maintain our circuitous route, and once, towards five in the morning, at the engineer's insistence, we halted at Ebensee to take on water. It was an operation that lasted some minutes, and a good deal of steam escaped into the pre-dawn air with a shriek and a shower of sparks, but the engineer was considerably relieved to have done it, and we gathered speed once more, contenting ourselves with the stationmaster's assurance that the Baron had no doubt encountered worse obstacles negotiating the big terminus at Linz.

Light was piercing the sky and brightening our way in orange and red streaks as we threw the last set of points at Bad Ischl, where the railway men stared in astonishment. then yelled after us as we roared through the station. Leaning out of the cab, I could see them scurrying in a dozen different directions like so many ants.

"They'll telegraph ahead." I prophesied. The stationmaster nodded heavily and threw out his hands in a gesture of helplessness.

"We must take that risk," Holmes decided, "there is nothing for it. Keep the throttle open, engineer!"

On we plunged, the sun rising behind us and some charming lakes glistening in its early rays to our right. Indeed, though we scarcely had time to admire it, the scenery repeated the magnificence I had observed passing through the district on our way to Vienna.

Now, however, instead of sitting idly in a comfortable compartment, gazing out of the window at the snowcapped peaks and philosophizing, I was in the act of breaking down a very similar window, whilst Holmes with other tools at his disposal from the engine cab was standing on the roof of the car, pulling it apart, piece by piece, and dropping it into a hole he had gouged for the purpose onto the aisle beneath. There Dr. Freud collected it and dumped it into the tender from where the stationmaster transferred it to our still-burning fire.

The city of Salzburg was in plain view, and I was adding my lot to the pile of debris in the corridor, when shouts from the engineer and stationmaster drew us to the front of the car.

Wonder of wonders! Not three miles off, as I should judge, a train was heading south-west, with an engine, a tender, and three cars in tow.

"There they are!" Holmes cried with satisfaction, his eyes gleaming. "Berger, you are a genius!" He gave the astonished stationmaster an enthusiastic hug, then paused to watch the train ahead of us cross the nose of our engine a mile or two away as it switched effortlessly into the line for Salzburg. If the Baron and his party saw our train, or suspected from its presence that anything was amiss, they gave no outward sign. A mile further and we were obliged to stop and change the last set of points to put ourselves directly in the wake of the Baron's special.

16

What Happened Next

"Now, we must pour on every ounce of steam we can," Sherlock Holmes ordered, cupping his hands to make himself heard, "and don't worry about the points. They have all been switched to accommodate the Baron's train, but we must catch them before they reach the frontier at the Salzach."

We had been exhausted moments before, each man on the point of collapse, but now, fired by the sight of our quarry, we did as Holmes bid and rushed frantically about, heaping the boiler fires higher and whiter than ever with the fragments of a once proud railway carriage. As we entered the city of Salzburg, the tracks branched before us into a labyrinth as complex as the bloodstream in a human body. If just one of these points had already been switched back we were dead men, and the engineer lost his nerve totally. His place was assumed at once by the lusty stationmaster, Berger, while the frightened man contented himself with timidly tossing pieces of wood into the stoke hold, no longer daring to look ahead.

Once again we drew near the Baron's train and

Holmes discharged the revolver into the air to gain their attention. It was a needless gesture for we had already been seen. I could perceive two heads sticking out the cab window, looking back at us, and moments later the Baron's engine picked up speed.

The city of Salzburg whipped past at a dizzying speed. I found—like the unfortunate engineer—that it did not pay to look too closely at the track. Nevertheless, it was impossible not to see the station rushing up at us as we roared through it, and the stares of amazement on the faces of the people there. The Baron's train was travelling at a far greater speed than was permitted by the rules of the station, but to watch another train hurtling through right behind it—this was clearly as astonishing as it was hazardous! I was dimly aware of whistles blowing (one of them was ours, pulled by Berger) and people yelling.

Once through the station it was only a matter of moments before the Baron's train reached the River Salzach and crossed into Bavaria. Oblivious to everything now, we scuttled the remains of that car faster than one would have supposed possible.

"They've closed the barriers!" Freud cried, pointing up ahead to the frontier, which the Baron's special had just passed through.

"Ram them," ordered Sherlock Holmes, and we did, sending a spray of wood and splinters in every direction.

In Bavaria now, our locomotive proved its worth, and we began gaining in earnest on the fugitive special. In pauses for breath we could see someone shaking a fist at us, and a moment later we heard shots.

"Down!" Holmes commanded, and we fell to the floor of the cab—all except the foolish engineer, who had chosen that moment to raise himself up for a look and took a bullet in the shoulder. He whirled back like a puppet yanked by a string and spun round against the tender. Holmes waved me over to him while he and Freud went back for more fuel. Crawling over to the unhappy man I ascertained that the wound was not a serious one, though painful. I staunched and bandaged it with what was available to me in my bag, but the removal of the bullet at this time was impossible. Our locomotive was trembling as though it had contracted palsy, and my scalpels had all been dulled beyond repair when they were appropriated for slitting seat covers.

Freud and Holmes returned with the last load of improvised fuel and deposited it in the fire, informing me that there was nothing left of the carriage that would succumb to flame. It was now or never. If our fires diminished, as it appeared they must, the game was lost.

"Turn loose the platform," the stationmaster suggested. "It will give us more speed."

Holmes nodded and, taking me with him, left Freud to look after the engineer. We climbed through the empty tender and stood over the naked couplings which connected it to the remains of the carriage, the ground rushing by below us at a fearful rate. Holmes straddled the huge iron claws while I got on my stomach and held him firmly around the waist.

First he threw off the heavy emergency links and then proceeded to undo the revolving bolts that pinned the car to the tender. Because of the great speed and deafening noise, it was difficult work, as I could tell by the expanding exertions of his chest. From my vantage point I saw nothing of his efforts, and my arms were beginning to ache with the strain of maintaining his precarious position, when there was a sudden release and a great burst of speed. Had I not been holding fast, Holmes would have toppled to an instant death.

As it was, I held tight and brought him slowly to the lip of the tender, an operation that seemed to take forever and one I should not gladly undertake again. When he had landed safe, Holmes nodded heavily and bent over to get his breath.

"Never let them say you were merely my Boswell, Watson," he gasped when he could speak. "Never let them say that."

I smiled and followed him as we clambered back through the tender for the last time, being careful going over the top, for someone was still squeezing off rounds in our general direction, though at this distance and rate the bullet that had struck our engineer had been a lucky one.

We succeeded in regaining the cab once more, and looked ahead. There could be no doubt of it; we were rapidly overtaking the Baron's train. I suggested releasing the tender as well, as there was nothing to burn left inside it, but Berger cautioned us that it served as ballast, and that at the speed we were making it would be dangerous to dispense with it.

Yet we had burned every scrap of flammable material at our disposal; we had released the iron wheels of our only carriage. There was nothing further to be done. If we did not now close in on that train, all our efforts had been in vain. I shuddered to think of the international repercussions caused by our blasting through the barriers at the frontier, to say nothing of the general manner in which we had flung down and danced upon every regulation in the rail manual. Destroying railway property, indeed!

Even as I watched, the needle on the pressure

gauge dropped from its hitherto constant position (some few degrees to the right of the red-labelled danger zone), and Holmes gave vent to a sigh that could be heard above the roar of the pistons and furnaces.

"We have lost," said he.

And so we would have, too, had not the Baron, in his eagerness to escape, made a fatal error. I was on the point of replying with some words of false cheer when my attention was caught by the rear carriage of the Baron's train, which seemed to be drawing nearer at an alarming rate.

"Holmes!" I pointed. "He has released one of his cars!" Berger had seen it almost at the same moment and he threw the sticks over as hard and quickly as he could. I felt our wheels freeze beneath us and saw sparks fly in every direction from the rails as we struggled to avoid a collision. For twenty agonizing seconds we squealed along with no evident diminution of speed, ever closer to the cast-off car. Everyone braced for the shock, and Freud held the wounded engineer, but at the last moment, we realized that we were not going to strike after all. The Baron had released the carriage on a downgrade, and, having been pulled along at a smart pace behind his locomotive, the vehicle had succumbed to the inevitable laws of momentum and was now travelling ahead of us through the mountains at a good clip, though indeed, slow enough to have sunk us had Berger not taken prompt and vigourous action.

Holmes, perceiving the situation, threw off his Inverness and started round the cab towards the front of the engine.

"Open it up!" he called. "We can join her!"

Berger hesitated a moment at the audacity of the plan, then nodded and eased open the throttle. The railings which ran along the boiler were too hot to hold, as I could tell, for Holmes was obliged to remove his Norfolk and was using it to shield his hands as he worked his way along the side of the heaving locomotive.

Freud, Berger, the engineer (who had got to his feet), and I watched with breathless anticipation as Holmes inched towards the nose of the engine whilst the Baron's discarded railway carriage again loomed into imminent perspective.

Berger, however, was a master craftsman, and nudged into the car as gently as could be expected, considering the rate at which both vehicles were travelling. There was a brief shock, but neither engine nor carriage jumped the rails, and as the downgrade became an upgrade, the car settled quite nicely against us.

From the nose of the engine, Holmes managed to step aboard. There he waved one of us to follow him. I started to go, but Freud held me by the arm.

"Your leg will not permit it," he yelled into my ear, and, removing his own jacket, he imitated Holmes's precautions and followed the detective's path.

He returned some moments later, carrying a sack of curtains which we threw into the fire, and a suggestion from Holmes, who was assembling more improvised fuel, that it might now be safe to release the tender. Berger agreed that it was now possible (though not advisable), and we set to work, soon completing this manoeuvre. Holmes returned with more items to burn and the needle on the pressure gauge began to rise. Thanks to the additional fuel and the loss of the tender, we were again gaining on the Baron's train. Holmes made his way over to Berger, who was busy with the controls and spoke intently into his ear. The man started back and stared at him, then shrugged, and clapped him on the shoulder. Holmes returned to where I stood and asked for the revolver.

"What will you do?" I said, handing it over.

"What I can," he answered, echoing Freud's words in response to a similar question. "Watson, old man, if we do not meet again, you will think kindly of me, I trust?"

"But Holmes—"

He gripped my hand with a pressure that stopped all words, then turned to Dr. Freud.

"Is this necessary?" Freud asked. Like myself, he appeared to have no notion of the detective's intentions, but his words had created an ominous impression.

"I am afraid it is," Holmes responded. "At all events, I can think of nothing else. Good-bye, Sigmund Freud, and may God bless you for the work you have done and for the services you will yet render Mankind: for saving my own wretched life, if for nothing more."

"I did not save it to assist you in casting it away again," Freud protested, and it seemed to me his eyes were watering, though this may merely have been the effect of the heat, the soot, and the wind.

In any case, Holmes did not hear him, for he was starting once more towards the car we were pushing before us, as the Baron's train drew nearer and nearer still. So engrossed were we in observing his progress that it was not until it was almost upon us that we perceived another train travelling in the opposite direction on the parallel set of tracks. Holmes, preoccupied with his footing, did not see it, nor was he able to hear our frantic shouts to pull himself in as it passed. The train so startled him as it roared by, a fraction from his body, that he let go one hand and was very nearly sucked into the tremendous vacuum. But he regained his hold and nodded to us with a jerky movement of his head that he was unhurt. The next instant he disappeared into the empty carriage.

Exactly what took place then is difficult to describe. I have seen it in my dreams, and even compared recollections with Freud on the subject, but it happened so quickly and amidst such confusion that the events blur in both our memories.

Berger was now overtaking the Baron's train at his own pace, and he eased the car we were pushing into the Baron's two remaining carriages. As we wound amongst those stupendous mountains, Berger duplicated the Baron's pace, imitating precisely the openings and closings of the other engine's throttle.

In this fashion we dashed into a tunnel, and in the blackness, shots were heard, echoing even above the din of the trains. In another instant we were thrust once more into open air. I could stand no more of the suspense, and, wound or no wound, determined to follow my friend. Freud knew it was useless to dissuade me this time, and together we started forward, when the engineer uttered a cry and pointed.

Someone was climbing on top of the nearest car! It was a man, dressed in black, wearing highly polished boots and holding a pistol in one hand and a sabre in the other.

"It's the Baron!" Freud exclaimed.

Oh, for my revolver! A weapon—anything! If he had slain Holmes and now intended to fire upon us, we were lost. Without the tender behind there was nothing to shelter us from his lethal perch on top of the car. At that moment, I believe I did not so much mind the thought of dying, as of dying without avenging Holmes.

Yet he was not dead! Even as we watched, a second figure emerged on the roof of the same carriage at the other end. It was Sherlock Holmes, and, like the Baron, he carried a revolver and a sabre, though how these weapons chanced to be aboard the train I did not learn until afterwards.

As we lurched through the magnificent Bavarian countryside, the two men faced each other at opposite ends of the car. They appeared almost motionless but for their efforts to retain their balance on top of the swaying carriage. It was one of those efforts that caused Holmes to lose his footing; as he stumbled. the Baron whipped round his revolver and fired. He had not reckoned with the same jolts that had caused Holmes to slip, however. Another shook him the instant he aimed and his shot went wide. He tried again as Holmes rose to his feet, but the gun would not discharge. Either it had no more bullets or its firing mechanism had jammed. With a furious gesture, he hurled it aside. In automatic response Holmes brought up his own weapon and aimed it.

But he did not fire.

"Holmes! Shoot! Shoot!" we called up to him. If he heard us he gave no sign. Nor did he pay any heed when we tried to warn him of the approaching tunnel behind him. The Baron held his ground while death, in the form of a stone arch, drew rapidly closer to the detective.

Ironically, it was the Baron who saved him. Seeing the tunnels, he lost his nerve and flattened himself on the roof of the car. In an instant Holmes divined the reason for this manoeuvre and did likewise, the gun flying from his hand as he went down.

This second tunnel seemed an eternity in length.

What were they doing up there? Was that fiend even now taking advantage of the darkness, and inching his way along the car with the object of stabbing my friend under its cover? One can go mad at such moments.

When we again burst into the daylight, we discerned the combatants moving towards one another, precariously balanced, swords in hand.

In an instant they grappled and their blades crossed, flashing in the clear sunlight. Back and forth they slashed and thrust, struggling to maintain their footing as they dueled. Neither was an amateur. The young Baron had been trained at Heidelberg—and had that pretty scar to show for it—and Holmes was an expert singlestick player as well as fencing champion. I had not seen him work with a sabre before, nor had I ever witnessed a contest of arms on more unlikely or treacherous ground.

Truth forces me to confess, however, that the Baron was Holmes's superior with the sabre. He pressed him slowly, relentlessly back to the end of the car, his satanic features grinning with eager anticipation as he perceived his advantage.

"Keep her close!" I yelled to Berger, and he opened the throttle—and not a second too soon. We rammed the Baron's train again, just as Holmes was compelled to retreat to it with a backward leap. Had we not been tight, he would have stepped into oblivion.

The Baron pursued him with an agility and grace that would have done justice to a jaguar, before Berger had time to adjust the throttle and separate them by slowing us down. Again Holmes stumbled and his opponent lost not a moment in lunging for him. The detective rolled to avoid the blow, but the Baron's blade found part of its mark, at least, and I saw blood spurt from his victim's exposed arm.

And then it was over. How it happened, or precisely what happened, I have never determined. Holmes himself says that he cannot remember, but it appears that in trying to pierce him a second time, the Baron drew back his blade, lost his footing, and impaled himself on Holmes's sword as the latter twisted round, point upraised, to rise again.

The Baron drew back with such force that the sabre hilt was wrenched from my friend's hand; yet so furiously had the villain rushed upon it that he was unable to pull it forth from his body. He stood for a moment on the carriage roof, swaying, his evil face immobile with shock, and then, with an awful cry—I still hear it sometimes in my dreams —he plunged over the side. Holmes remained on his knees for some moments, clutching his arm and striving not to roll off. Then he looked about and down at us.

Freud and I scrambled from the engine as hastily as we dared, and climbed to the top of the car. There we got hold of him and carefully worked him down the ladder at the other end. Freud wanted to examine the wound, but Holmes shook his head stubbornly, insisting that it was only a scratch, and led us through the two cars still connected with the Baron's speeding train. In the first of these we came upon the prostrate body of the large butler, struck through the temple by a bullet fired by Holmes when he had entered the car. Crouching in one corner, screaming in uncontrolled hysterics, which distorted her every magnificent feature, was the woman who had so convincingly personated the Baroness Von Leinsdorf. She did not move as we made our way through, but sat sobbing like a child in a pet, rocking herself frantically to and fro. The carriage itself was sumptuously appointed with the same lavish trappings that had been characteristic of the Baron's Vienna mansion. On the walls, alternating between the windows and draperies, were armourial mementos, and it was from one of these gilded crests that Holmes and the Baron had seized their weapons. We paused to gape at the splendid interior of the vehicle, but Holmes urged us on.

"Hurry!" he pleaded in weakening tones. "Hurry!"

We crossed into the first car, which contained the baggage, and a great deal of it there proved to be. In desperate haste, supervised by the detective, we began our search amongst innumerable trunks and portmanteaus.

"Look for the air holes," Holmes panted, leaning on his sabre and clutching the barred window for support.

"Here!" exclaimed Freud abruptly. He seized the sword and slid its blade behind the lock of an enormous trunk. With a mighty effort he tore loose the catch, and he and I together threw back the clasps and forced the thing open on its massive hinges.

And there, alive, unharmed, and in much the same condition we had left her—her blue-grey eyes open but unseeing—sat Nancy Osborn Slater Von Leinsdorf.

Sherlock Holmes stared down at her for some moments, swaying slightly.

"No backhand," he murmured, and then, after a pause, "Let us stop these trains—" before falling into my arms.

17

The Final Problem

"We have not really prevented a war," Sherlock Holmes observed, setting aside his brandy. "The most we can be said to have done is postponed it."

"But—"

"It is no secret that fleets are building up at Scapa Flow," he returned with a touch of impatience, though not unkindly, "and if the Kaiser wishes to go to war with Russia over the Balkans, he will find the means to do so. With the Baron dead and the Baroness incapable, it would not astonish me to learn that the German government has declared the will null and the estates intestate. At that time," he twisted round in his chair to face Freud, being careful not to disarrange the sling which supported his left arm, "you and I, Doctor, may find ourselves on opposing sides."

We were back once more in the familiar study at Bergasse 19, though this was destined to be our last visit to that comfortable room, whose smoke-filled atmosphere had, of late, increasingly reminded me of Holmes's Baker Street digs.

Sigmund Freud shook his head in melancholy

agreement, when Holmes had finished speaking, and lit another cigar.

"It was partially to prevent that situation that I helped you, yet I cannot doubt the truth of your prophecy." He sighed. "Perhaps all our labours have availed nothing."

"I should not go quite that far." Holmes smiled and again adjusted his position in the chair. The wound in his arm was not without complications, for the Baron's blade had pinked a nerve, and every movement was painful. With a great effort he held his pipe in his left hand, slowly bringing it up to his lips, where he lit it and allowed it to remain, easing his hand slowly down again. "We have, after all, gained time, and that is the essential good to be derived from our efforts. You recall Marvell's choice phrase, Watson? 'Had we world enough and time'?" He turned slightly to face me. "Well, what the world needs desperately is time. Given time, perhaps humanity will come to grips with that terrible half of itself that seems always bent on useless acts of waste and devastation. If our work has gained but an hour more in which to understand the human predicament, it shall not have been in vain."

"There are other benefits of a more immediate nature to show for our work," I assured both men. "For one thing, we have rescued that unfortunate woman from a fate worse than death, and for another—" I hesitated and stopped in confusion. Holmes laughed gently and continued my train of thought for me.

"And for another, Dr. Freud has saved my life. Had I not come to Vienna, and had your cure not been successful, sir, I should doubtless have missed this and every other intriguing little problem that may ever chance to come my way. And," he added, taking up his glass once more, "had you, Watson, not contrived to get me here against my will, Dr. Freud would never have had the opportunity to save a doomed addict. To both of you, in fact, I owe my life. To Watson, here, there will be a lifetime to repay the debt, but to you, Doctor, I confess I am at a loss. If my predictions are accurate, this may be the last time we see one another for some—perhaps all—time. How can I repay you?"

Sigmund Freud did not respond at once. He had smiled in his inimitable way while Holmes was speaking. Now he tapped an ash from his cigar and regarded my friend fixedly.

"Let me have a minute to think about it," he requested.

Our bags were packed; the case was closed. The Baron was dead and soon I should be back in London with my wife. The personator of Baroness Von Leinsdorf proved to be—as Holmes suspected— an American actress who had remained on the Continent after the return of her touring company. Her true name was Diana Marlowe and during the company's sojourn in Berlin she had met and been seduced by the young Baron. She was released after signing a statement tantamount to a confession (in which she acknowledged her illicit liaison) and also affixing her name to a document in which she swore never to reveal the events in which she had taken part, nor the names of any of the principals involved, including that of Sherlock Holmes. In addition, she was pledged never to return either to Austria or Germany.

The police authorities of two countries were anxious to hush up a scandal of major proportions, a near international incident. The facts had quickly become clear; Berger and the wounded engineer gave their depositions, and like ourselves were instructed to remain forever silent. The energetic sergeant of the Viennese Constabulary and his men were enjoined to similar oaths of discretion, though it was abundantly clear to all concerned that there was really no choice or motive other than to keep silent. The perpetrators of this wicked scheme had come to their just end, and as it might be some time (if ever) before the Baroness spoke again, the governments of the Emperor and the Kaiser doubtless deemed it prudent that their political machinations and alliances should not be made public at the present time and under these sordid circumstances. In point of fact, I later learned that it was not the old Emperor at all, but his scheming nephew, the Archduke Franz Ferdinand, who had entered into the cabal with Count Von Schlieffen, Baron Von Leinsdorf and the chancellery in Berlin. In an odd way, the Archduke was granted his terrible munitions: Germany presented them *carte blanche* to Austria after he had been assassinated at Sarajevo many years later, and the war that ensued cost the Kaiser his throne. I often thought, during those dark years that opened this century, of Sigmund Freud's brief interior profile of the man, based on the observation of his withered arm, though whether he was right or wrong in his conclusions I cannot say. As I noted earlier in this narrative, there were many points upon which we disagreed utterly.

As we were packing, Holmes and I naturally discussed the idea of violating our agreements with these two petty powers and revealing to the world their scandalous conduct. Once we were back in England there was nothing to prevent our doing so; our stolen train, the butler Holmes had slain, and the border we had violated could not be used— which they were while we remained in Austria

—as inducements to cooperate. Perhaps the world ought to know what mischief great men were planning for it.

Yet we decided to remain silent. We were not certain what the result of such revelations would be—neither of us being politically astute enough to gauge their importance—and, what was more, we could not reveal the truth of the matter without also revealing the complicity of Dr. Freud. And this, as he continued to reside in Vienna, we were loath to do.

"I'll tell you what I should like," Freud said at last, putting down his cigar and gazing steadfastly at Holmes. "I should like to hypnotize you once more."

I had no idea what he might ask (some part of me suspected that he would waive any such offer on Holmes's part altogether), but I had never expected this. No more than Holmes, who blinked in surprise and coughed before replying.

"You wish to hypnotize me? For what purpose?"

Freud shrugged, retaining the same quiet smile.

"You spoke just now of the human predicament," said he. "I must confess it is my overpowering interest. And as it has been observed that the proper study of mankind is man, I thought you might permit me to peer once more into your brains."

Holmes considered the request briefly.

"Very well. I am your willing subject."

"Shall I go?" I asked, rising to leave the room if Freud believed my presence might interfere with the proceedings.

"I should prefer you to remain," he answered, drawing the curtains and fetching forth his fob yet again.

It was an easier task to hypnotize the detective now than it had been in the past when we had so desperately relied on Freud's technique for successfully weaning him from cocaine. Now that the proper rapport was established, there was nothing to cloud either of their minds, and plenty of time. Holmes closed his eyes within three minutes and sat immobile, awaiting the doctor's instructions.

"I am going to ask you some questions," he began, talking in a low and gentle voice, "and you will answer them. When we are finished, I will snap my fingers and you will awaken. When you do, you will remember nothing that has taken place whilst you were asleep. Do you understand?"

"Perfectly."

"Very well." He took a breath. "When did you first use cocaine?"

"At the age of twenty."

"Where?"

"At University."

"Why?"

There was no answer.

"Why?"

"Because I was unhappy."

"Why did you become a detective?"

"To punish the wicked and see justice done."

"Have you ever known injustice done?"

There was a pause.

"Have you?" Freud repeated, licking his lips and eyeing me briefly.

"Yes."

I had resumed my seat and was listening to this exchange with the utmost attention and fascination, my hands propped upon my knees, my body thrust forward as I strained to hear the soft replies.

"Have you known wickedness personally?"

"Yes."

"What was this wickedness?"

Again the subject hesitated and again he was encouraged to answer.

"What was this wickedness?"

"My mother deceived my father."

"She had a lover?"

"Yes."

"What was the injustice?"

"My father killed her."

Sigmund Freud straightened up with a start and looked wildly about the room for an instant, as totally out of control as myself, for I had risen to my feet in automatic response, then froze, though my eyes and ears still functioned. Freud recovered more quickly than I, however, and bent down once more to the subject.

"Your father murdered your mother?" *

"Yes." The voice choked back a sob that split my heart as I heard it.

"And her lover?" Freud persisted, his own eyes beginning to blink rapidly.

"Yes."

Freud paused in order to collect himself before going on.

"Who was—"

"Doctor!" I cut him off and he looked at me.

"What is it?"

"Do not—do not ask him to reveal the man's name, I beg you. It can mean nothing to anyone now."

Freud hesitated a moment, then nodded.

"Thank you."

He nodded again and returned to Holmes, who had sat motionless, his eyes closed, throughout this

---

* This amazing event was actually deduced by Trevor Hall in his essay, "The Early Years of Sherlock Holmes," included in his masterly volume, *Sherlock Holmes—Ten Literary Studies*, St. Martin's Press, 1969.

digression. Only the sudden appearance of perspiration beads on his forehead served to indicate his inner torment.

"Tell me," Freud resumed, "how did you learn what your father had done?"

"My tutor informed me."

"Professor Moriarty?"

"Yes."

"He broke the news?"

"Yes."

"I see." Freud drew out his watch fob and stared at it for some moments, then put it away again. "All right, sleep now, Herr Holmes. Sleep. Sleep. I will awaken you shortly and you will remember nothing, *nothing* of this interview. Do you understand?"

"I said that I did."

"Good. Sleep now."

Watching for some moments and ascertaining that he did not move, Freud rose once more and crossed the room, pulling up a chair close to mine. His eyes were sadder than ever. He said nothing as he clipped and lighted another cigar. I had sunk back into my own chair, my brain in a whirl and my ears roaring with the shock.

"A man does not turn to narcotics because it is the fashion or because he likes it," he said at length, squinting at me through the smoke of his cigar. "You remember I once asked you how he had been introduced to the drug, and not only were you unable to answer, you did not at the time perceive the importance of my question. Yet I knew from the first that something had provoked his dangerous practise."

"But—" I cast a look in Holmes's direction, "did you dream—?"

"No, I did not. I never imagined anything like

what we have just heard. Yet as he would himself observe: see how much is explained by these facts. Now we not only understand the origin of the addiction and the reason he adopted his chosen profession; we also comprehend his aversion to women and the difficulty he has in dealing with them. Further, his antipathy to Moriarty is explained. Like the Persian messengers of old who bore bad news, Moriarty is punished for his role in the affair, negligible though it appears to have been. In your friend's mind, under the influence of saturating cocaine, Moriarty becomes part of the illicit liaison and is guilty by association. Not merely guilty," here he leaned forward and gestured with the cigar for emphasis, "but *supremely* guilty! Lacking a genuine scapegoat for his pain, Herr Holmes pins the outrage itself on the man who has disclosed it. Of course all these conclusions he buries deep in his soul—in an area to which I have tentatively applied the clinical term 'unconscious'—never admitting any of these feelings to himself, but exhibiting the symptoms of his ideas, nevertheless— in his choice of profession, in his indifference to women (so well recorded by you, Doctor!), and finally in his preference for the drug under whose influence his true, innermost feelings on the subject are eventually to be revealed."

In less time than it takes to report it, I had grasped the stupendous truth in Sigmund Freud's assertion. This also explained Mycroft Holmes's equally eccentric withdrawal from the world, to a place where even speech was forbidden, and both brothers' commitment to eternal bachelorhood. Of course Professor Moriarty had somewhere in this business played a larger part than the one Freud had assigned him (this accounted for Mycroft

Holmes's hold over him), but over all, I knew the doctor was correct.

"You are the greatest detective of all." I could think of nothing else to say.

"I am not a detective." Freud shook his head, smiling his sad, wise smile. "I am a physician whose province is the troubled mind." It occurred to me that the difference was not great.

"And what can we do for my friend?"

He sighed and shook his head again.

"Nothing."

"Nothing?" I was stunned. Had he led me this far only to go no further?

"Nothing. I do not know how to get at these feelings other than through the clumsy and inefficient device of hypnosis."

"But why inefficient?" I protested, my hand grasping his sleeve. "Surely—"

"Because the patient in this case would be unwilling—I may say unable—to accept its testimony when conscious. He would not believe me. He would not believe you. He would say we were lying."

"But—"

"Come now, Doctor. If you had not been here and witnessed it yourself, would you have believed it?"

I confessed that I would not.

"Well, therein lies our problem. In any case, it is doubtful whether or not he would remain here long enough for us to work our way down to those innermost depths by any other route. Already he is in haste to depart."

We argued the matter for several minutes, but I knew from the first that he was right. Whatever techniques would help Sherlock Holmes, they were yet to be discovered.

"You must take heart," Freud enjoined me.

"Your friend, after all, is a functioning human being. He performs noble work and performs it well. Within the framework of his unhappiness, he is nevertheless successful and even beloved.

"Someday perhaps science will unravel the mysteries of the human mind," he concluded, "and when that day comes I have no doubt that Sherlock Holmes will be as responsible for its arrival as anyone else—whether or not his own brain is ever relieved of its terrible burden."

Then we both fell silent for a time, after which Freud roused the detective from his trance. As he had been directed, he recalled nothing.

"Did I tell you anything of importance?" Holmes enquired, relighting his pipe.

"I am afraid it was not terribly exciting," the hypnotist told him, smiling. I contrived to be looking in another direction as he said this, while Holmes rose and circled the room for the last time, running his eye eagerly over the countless volumes.

"What will you do for the Baroness?" he asked, coming forward again and reaching for his Inverness.

"What I can."

They smiled, and shortly thereafter we made our farewells to the rest of the household; to Paula, to Frau Freud, and to little Anna, who wept copiously as she waved good-bye to our cab with a tear-stained handkerchief. Holmes called out a promise that someday he would return and play the violin for her again.

Throughout the ride to the station, however, he relapsed into a thoughtful silence. He remained in such a brown study that I did not like to disturb him, though his sudden alteration of mood surprised and worried me. Nevertheless, I felt bound to tell him when we arrived that he had led us to the platform of the Milan Express. He smiled at me and shook his head.

"I'm afraid there is no mistake, Watson," said he.

"But the Dover train is—"

"I am not returning to England."

"Not returning?"

"Not just yet. I think that I need a little time to myself, a little time to think—and, yes, to pull myself together. You go on without me."

"But—" I floundered, stunned by this turn of events, "when will you return?"

"One day," he replied vaguely. "In the meantime," he added, coming to life, "inform my brother of my decision and ask him to tell Mrs. Hudson that my rooms are to be maintained as always and not to be touched. Is that clear?"

"Yes, but—" It was no use; he was travelling much too fast for me. I looked helplessly about the busy terminus, furious with my own inability to deal with him in this humour and wishing desperately that Freud were here.

"My dear fellow," said he not unkindly, holding me by the arm, "you mustn't take it so hard. I tell you I am going to recover. But I need time. It may be a long time." After a pause, he went on hastily. "But I shall return to Baker Street, you have my word. Please give my best to Mrs. Watson," he concluded, pressing my hand warmly as he stepped onto the Milan train, which had begun to roll slowly out of the station.

"But Holmes, how will you live? Have you any money?" I was walking beside the train, the length of my limping stride increasing with each step.

"Not much," he admitted, smiling down cheerfully, "but I do have my violin and I think I may be able to support myself in more ways than one when my arm has mended." He chuckled. "If you wish to keep track of my whereabouts, simply follow the concert career of a violinist named Sigerson." He shrugged with his good shoulder. "And if that should fail me, why then I shall wire Mycroft for a draft."

"But—" I was running alongside the train now— "what about your readers—*my* readers! What shall I tell them?"

"Anything you like," was the bland reply. "Tell them I was murdered by my mathematics tutor, if you like. They'll never believe you in any case."

Then the train steamed off at a pace my failing legs could not hope to manage.

My own trip back to England was uneventful. I slept most of the way, and when I stepped off the platform at Victoria, there was my own dear girl waiting for me with a wide smile and open arms.

And it will surprise no one to learn that when it came time to write down what had occurred, I followed Sherlock Holmes's advice to the letter.

Acknowledgements

It is my happy task to take the reader of this book behind the scenes and to express my gratitude to the writers, critics, and friends whose works or suggestions directly influenced the shape and outcome of *The Seven-Per-Cent Solution*.

First and foremost, I am overwhelmingly in debt to the genius of the late Sir Arthur Conan Doyle, who created in Sherlock Holmes and Dr. Watson the most popular characters in fiction. Without Doyle, this book could not have been thought of, let alone written.

Readers who are not Sherlock Holmes *aficionados* are doubtless unaware of the tremendous bibliography of Holmesian criticism, a wealth of literature that fills hundreds of volumes. These light-hearted speculations on the part of some brilliant writers were responsible for putting the idea of this book into my head in the first place, and some of their most imaginative theories I have endeavoured to intertwine and incorporate into the book's plot. I should like to acknowledge my chief sources of inspiration.

Among these "Sherlockians" (as they are termed in the United States), the late William S. Baring-Gould, author of a wonderful biography of the detective, *Sherlock Holmes of Baker Street,* and editor of the stupendous two-volume annotated collection of the complete Holmes stories, may be said to have performed the function of Head Muse. It was Baring-Gould's contention that Professor Moriarty tutored young Sherlock in mathematics.

More recently, Trevor Hall, in his indispensable work, *Sherlock Holmes—Ten Literary Studies,* deduced the adulterous affair of the detective's mother and her subsequent murder by his father, a family history that very conveniently explains a great many aspects of Holmes's character, including his profession.

Psychiatrist Dr. David F. Musto, in a brilliant essay published in *Journal of the American Medical Association* plausibly connected Holmes with Dr. Sigmund Freud through the all-important link of cocaine, and Irving L. Jaffee, in his slim volume, *Elementary, My Dear Watson,* also suggested to my mind a relationship between Holmes and Freud.

For Victorian history and descriptions of the world and era of Sherlock Holmes, I am obliged to Michael Harrison, whose excellent *In the Footsteps of Sherlock Holmes* and *The London of Sherlock Holmes* are delightful and informative reading even to those who have never read any of the famous detective's exploits.

I am further indebted to the close scrutiny of several friends and relatives, whose encouragement and sharp-eyed criticism kept me going and as accurate as possible where details of Holmesiana were concerned. Sean Wright, Chairman of the Los Angeles Sherlock Holmes Society (*The Non-Canonical Calabashes*), made many important suggestions and corrections, as did Craig Fisher, Michael Pressman, and Michael Scheff, as well as my cousins in Fresno—the entire Winston Strong family—and my father, Dr. Bernard C. Meyer of New York City.

Deepest thanks are also extended to Ruth Notkins Nathan and Harriet F. Pilpel, without whose assistance the publication of this book would not have been possible.

Finally, my special thanks and appreciation are extended to Ms. Sally Welch Conner, whose unremitting enthusiasm for the project was really responsible for my actually writing the book. She also proof-read and typed the manuscript, and threw in the title—at no extra charge.

6 classic mysteries starring Raymond Chandler's hard-boiled hero

Together with Dashiell Hammett, Chandler is credited as the inventor of the modern crime story. Here are savage, fast-moving stories of tough men and beautiful lost women in the tawdry neon wilderness of Southern California — by the master of detective fiction.

TIM HEALD

is the creator
of *Simon Bognor,*
the sleuth who's as bumbling
as Clouseau
and as canny as Poirot.